MAGGIE ROSE AND SASS

MAGGIE ROSE AND SASS

by

Eunice Boeve

Rowe Publishing

ISBN 13: 978-1-939054-21-0
ISBN 10: 1-939054-21-4

Cover Photo Credits:

Girl portrayed as "Maggie Rose" is Elizabeth Leiker, photo by Emily Leiker, Hays, Kansas.

Girl portrayed as "Sass" and town photo are courtesy of Nicodemus Historical Society Collection, Spencer Research Library, Libraries at the University of Kansas.

A Kansas Notable Book

1 3 5 7 9 8 6 4 2

Printed in the United States of America
Published by

Rowe Publishing

www.rowepub.com
Stockton, Kansas

FOR MY GRANDDAUGHTER
ALLYSON
AND MY FRIEND
ANGELA

~ *Chapter One* ~

MAGGIE ROSE

The sound startled Maggie Rose. She snapped her book shut and sat up straighter on her bed. *Had something fallen in Grandmother's room?* She was certain Grandmother was still in there, in the bedroom next to hers. Even if she had gone downstairs, she would have heard the old woman's muttered complaints as she eased her bulky body down the winding stairway, her ancient liver-spotted hands gripping the railing. Maybe Hattie had made the noise. But in all the years she'd known the colored woman, and that had been all her twelve years of life, Maggie Rose had never heard her so much as rattle a pan or let a door slam back into place. No, Hattie Smith, when she moved through the house doing her work, made no more noise than a puff of smoke. Besides, she suddenly remembered, this was Sunday and Hattie's day off. If anyone checked on Grandmother today, it would have to be her.

She wished Hattie were here. She got paid for putting up with Grandmother's crankiness. In the days of slavery Hattie had waited on Grandmother hand and foot with no reward but a place to sleep and food to eat. Now she was free and getting paid, but she was also free to find work someplace else, so she must not mind putting up with the old woman.

Probably nothing was wrong. Most likely Grandmother had just dropped something. Since she had quit coming to the table, Hattie had brought Grandmother's meals up to her room. Except on Sundays, Hattie's day off. Then it was Maggie Rose's chore.

Grandmother had been all right when she brought her dinner to her at noon. It was nearly five o'clock now. She'd have to bring her some supper within the hour. Surely she could wait that long. No sense getting yelled at and called clumsy and stupid more times in a day than was necessary. Her decision made, Maggie Rose picked up her book and began to read, but this time she could not lose herself in the pages of this one of five books, her teacher, Miss Green, had loaned her for the summer. She sighed, pushed the book back up under her pillow, and slid off the faded, pink-flowered counterpane of her four-poster bed.

One day she had confided to Miss Green that she had read and reread her father's books shelved in a small bookcase in the attic, and that she wished somehow she'd discover one she hadn't yet read. How surprised and delighted she had been when Miss Green began bringing books from her family's library to school for Maggie Rose to take home and read. At first, getting the books past Grandmother's snooping nose had taken some doing. It was no problem now since Grandmother's last bout of illness kept her, most of the time, in her room. She was certain Grandmother would not have allowed her to accept Miss Green's generosity. She was quite sure that generosity was something beyond Grandmother's understanding. So as she read Miss Green's books, Maggie Rose kept an ear tuned to the sound of her grandmother's shuffling footsteps.

It didn't happen often now, since Grandmother had taken to her room, but she still might, without warning, yank open the door to Maggie Rose's room and step inside, her sharp old eyes scanning every nook and cranny, as if, Maggie Rose thought, partly in amusement and partly in anger, they were back in the times of the war and she was sure her granddaughter was hiding a "Yankee soldier."

For Grandmother, the War Between the States was a constant memory. Even now in 1888, twenty-three years since the South's surrender, the war in which she'd lost her husband and had set the coloreds free, still lived on in her mind.

On stocking feet, Maggie Rose crossed her room and stepped out into the hallway. The drone of a fly against the windowpane, above the stairway, was the only sound in the quiet stillness of the house.

The other bedrooms along the hallway were empty. Hattie slept downstairs, and Grandmother's three children had been gone now for years. Edward, the eldest son and Maggie Rose's father, had died six years ago. He had been Grandmother's favorite and had lived with her all his life, even after he married. Grandmother had disowned her daughter, Susan, when she married a man Grandmother called "a piece of trash." The youngest child, a son named Caleb, lived out west in Kansas in a town called Solomon Town, where he ran a general store and had a wife and several children. He wrote to Grandmother once a year and sent money to her lawyer for their keep. Each year Grandmother answered his letter, promising him the moon if he'd come back to Georgia. Not that she had the moon to offer. The truth was she was penniless and it was Uncle Caleb's money that kept her in this big, old house Grandfather Goodwin had inherited from his father and had brought her to as a bride.

3

Maggie Rose knew her father had been Grandmother's favorite, and that his death had turned her already sour disposition into bitter anger towards life. Once, after Grandmother had yelled at Hattie about some cleaning not done to her liking, and had stomped off, Maggie Rose, sunk deep in an overstuffed chair and unseen by either of them, had heard Hattie mutter, *"Her soul must belong to the devil. Sure do wish Mr. Edward be here to keep her half fit to live with."*

Even after six years, Maggie Rose still missed her father and, in a way, she missed her mother too. Her mother had died giving her birth, and Maggie Rose had learned the strange truth that you could miss, quite terribly, what you have never had, and she had shed many tears wishing for a mother's gentle voice and loving arms.

Hattie always said of folks who'd passed on, *"They gone to their eternal reward. Can't no thing be hurtin' them now."* Maggie Rose's parents were buried in the Goodwin plot beside Grandfather Goodwin under the sheltering branches of a giant oak. Grandfather Goodwin had died in the War Between the States. *"Killed,"* Grandmother often said, her eyes flashing with anger, *"by a blue-bellied Yankee's bullet."*

Grandmother always said Maggie Rose's father was the very image of Grandfather Goodwin. Once, Maggie Rose asked whom she favored. Grandmother had answered in a tone of voice that spoke her anger and hate louder than any words, *"That woman your father married."*

There were no pictures of her mother in the house, and Maggie Rose had looked at her own image several dozen times trying to see how it could be so bad to look like her mother. Then one day she asked Hattie for her opinion.

"My, yes, child. I think you gonna be tall like your daddy. Otherwise, I don't see a speck of him in you." Hattie had paused in washing the dishes, her hands idle in the soapy water as she looked at her. "But you sure do favor Miss Amanda, you do. She was just awful pretty. Her hair long and straight and heavy, a honey-brown, same as yours. And her eyes, Lord, girl, she had beautiful eyes! Just clear and blue, a shade darker'n a robin's egg." Hattie had sighed heavily before adding, "She weren't more'n a girl, poor little thing. But she sure knowed how to treat folks. She surely did."

Hattie's words had brought tears to Maggie Rose's eyes, and often now she whispered to her own face in the mirror, imagining it was her mother's. How she wished she could have known her mother, even for a little while, so she would have some memories of her. She treasured the memories of her father. Although the image of his face had dimmed as she'd grown older, her memories of him were still clear. She used to wait for him to come home in the evening from his newspaper shop, standing on a chair, her nose pressed against the windowpane. When she'd see him turn the corner, she'd jump from the chair, run to meet him, and walk back with him—her hand in his.

Born in this room she now slept in, Maggie Rose had lived all her life in this house of Grandmother's. Before her father's death, it had been home—the six years since, simply shelter.

Now she stood before Grandmother's door, and the silent stillness of the house raised a sudden fear, touching her as if with a clammy hand. She shivered and bit down on her fingernails. The raw pain brought tears to her eyes.

She couldn't remember when she'd started biting her nails, and now, even though they were bitten to the quick and constantly sore, she could not stop. Grandmother called the habit low-bred and nasty, but the old woman couldn't do anything about it, for she couldn't very well pull out her fingernails, could she? That thought brought a rush of anger and she muttered to herself, *"If she's fallen she can just lay there and stew 'til she turns purple. Supper's not far off anyway."*

She turned and started back to her room, but her feet only carried her a few paces before her conscience stopped her. "All right," she muttered to herself, "I'll go in there, but I sure hope I don't set her off into one of her fits." It seemed as if most anything set her grandmother off these days. Maggie Rose would never forget the Sunday when Grandmother, forgetting it was Hattie's day off, had stormed out of the kitchen where she had expected to find the colored woman, and grabbing Maggie Rose's arm, had set off for the colored part of town.

Maggie Rose had tried to tell her it was Sunday, but when Grandmother was in one of her rages, a rabid dog listened better than she did, and probably could be stopped easier, too.

They had gone down the back roads to the colored part of town in a hired hack, pulled by a dapple-gray horse, to the house where Hattie spent her Sundays. Colorful flowers bloomed along the dirt path that led to the weathered house, its roof shrouded in the mossy branches of an old half-dead tree.

The driver wrapped the long, leather driving lines around the brake and half raised out of his seat, probably to help them out of the buggy, when Grandmother's angry voice ripped through the hot summer air, "Hattie Smith! You get your black behind out here, right this instant!"

Slowly the man eased himself back down on the seat and waited.

Maggie Rose, certain every colored in this cluster of tumble-down houses now peered from doorways and window panes, fought the impulse to slide down out of sight on the buggy's wooden floor.

"Get a bunch of coloreds together," Grandmother had told her many times, "and they'd as soon slit your throat as look at you." And not only were they capable of slitting your throat on a whim, according to Grandmother, but stupid, lazy, ungrateful creatures besides.

When there was no response from her first words, Grandmother yelled again. "I said, get your lazy, black behind out here, Hattie Smith. You hear me?"

Tall and thin, with movements that always reminded Maggie Rose of a willow swaying in a gentle breeze, Hattie stepped out of the doorway, raising a hand against the glare of the summer sun. "Y'all be needin' something, Miss Pearl?" she asked.

Grandmother's answer had made their driver visibly flinch. "Yes! I'm needing you to get your prissy, black self back to work. That's what I'm needing."

"It's Sunday," Hattie said. "Don't you recall I be off Sundays, Miss Pearl?"

"Sunday..." Grandmother's voice weakened and for a moment seemed tinged with fear. Fear? *Grandmother?* But the next moment Maggie Rose decided she must have heard wrong for her grandmother's old, angry voice again whipped out through the air and lashed at Hattie Smith, like a blacksnake in the hands of a mule-driving freight man.

"You worthless piece of black trash," she roared. "Sunday or no Sunday, you don't go a twitching your tail down here to this stinking mudwaller without giving me a by-your-leave. You hear me, Hattie Smith?"

"Yes'm, I do, Miss Pearl." Hattie's voice had stayed soft and calm, as if answering a pleasant tone of voice instead of one that shrilled like a banshee.

Maggie Rose wondered if all that hate she'd imagined behind the doors and windows of this place had dissolved into laughter at an old white woman who didn't even know it was Sunday.

"This heat be somethin' awful, Miss Pearl." Hattie's voice was now filled with gentle concern. "You best be gettin' on to home 'fore it gets any hotter. Miss Maggie Rose can make you some cool lemonade, and then you lie down for a spell 'til you gets to feelin' better."

"Well…" All that boiling steam of anger had seeped right out of Grandmother, but she had managed one last command. "All right! But you be sure to be back to make my breakfast in the morning."

Grandmother, silent on the way home, had gone immediately to her room. But she had left behind a loneliness as solid as a physical presence to follow Maggie Rose throughout the rest of the day. That day, even a book could not erase the feeling of hopelessness within her.

Although Maggie Rose loved books—stories that took her out of herself and this lonely old house—she would gladly give them up in exchange for a friend. She envied the girls she saw at school, laughing and talking and whispering among themselves. How she would love to have a friend, but she knew she could not—not as long as she lived with Grandmother.

With a heavy sigh, Maggie Rose raised her hand and knocked at Grandmother's door. "Are you awake, Grandmother?" she called. There was no answer. She swallowed hard, reached for the doorknob, twisted and pushed. For a second the shock was so great she couldn't move. Then she screamed and backed out of the doorway. Turning, she ran down the hallway and straight into the arms of Hattie who had just come up the stairs.

"Somethin' be wrong, Miss Maggie Rose?" Hattie was holding her by the arms and peering down into her face. "Somethin' happen to Miss Pearl?"

Maggie Rose could only nod, her eyes still full of the image of Grandmother sprawled on her back on her bedroom floor, her arms flung wide, her mouth agape, her eyes wide and staring.

"Thought so," Hattie said. "Kept thinkin' about you two here all alone. Kept feelin' somethin' be wrong. Figure it be best if I come on back."

~ *Chapter Two* ~

SASS

"Sass! Sass! Papa's home!" Sass looked up as her sister came around to the back of the house. Coming up from the garden where she had just helped herself to a tasty carrot straight from the ground, the soil rubbed off on her long, brown skirts, Sass had stopped to watch a bull snake slither along, looking, she supposed, for its breakfast.

"Oh, and you never gonna guess what else," Jo said, her pretty face alive with excitement.

"You're not going to Prairie City with us?" Sass said, grinning.

"Don't tease." Jo pouted a moment, and then remembering her news, brightened. "Papa say a white girl, just your age, gonna be coming to Solomon Town."

"A white girl? Where is she coming from?" Sass frowned in disbelief.

"She's Caleb Goodwin's niece. Her grandmother died, so she's coming here. Ain't that gonna be something? Having a white girl in our town?"

"Don't be saying *ain't*," Sass said. "Papa don't want us saying ain't."

Jo frowned. "I know. I forgot."

Sass looked at her older sister standing in front of her, her hands on her hips, elbows stuck out like wings, the rays of the morning sun making a kind of halo around her. She grinned. "Guess what I was watching?"

"I don't know," Jo said. "What was you watching anyway?"

"A snake," Sass said, a grin lighting her face.

Immediately, Jo took a step backward, her eyes, now as big as plates, scanning the grass all around her. "I don't know if you be teasing me or not," she said, anger rising in her voice, "but I'm going back to help Mama and Annie get things ready. You'd better be coming, too, or Mama's gonna be giving you a good talking to, girl."

Just before she disappeared back around the house, Jo turned and called out, "Why you watching snakes and awful things like that, anyhow? You be actin' more two than twelve. Don't know what you gonna amount to, if you don't start pretty soon to get civilized."

Sass laughed. On Thursday evenings, after he got the *Solomon Gazette* out, Papa always brought the paper home, and after supper he'd read it to them and afterwards talk about something he'd written. This week, Papa had an article about two men who had consumed too much liquor, and one had killed the other. In the article, he commended the citizens of Solomon Town for banning the sale of alcohol, except for medical use. In a "civilized" society, he had written, alcohol should be dispensed sparingly.

The word "civilized" had appealed to Jo, and whenever she found a word she liked, she nearly used it to death. And "civilized" was probably not how she saw her sister. She couldn't understand at all why Sass would rather be outside, even preferring to pull weeds in the garden than to be in the house sewing or cooking. She often fussed at poor Mama about it. Not that it ever bothered Mama. She usually just laughed. The last time, though, when Jo complained, Mama frowned and shook her head. "You two girls about alike as biscuits and cake," she'd said. "Though both be good eating."

Sass wondered why Jo was always fussing and going on like she was nearer forty than fourteen. Jo was the prettiest girl in Solomon Town, but she was so pale-skinned she could easily pass for white. She wondered if Jo didn't wish to look more colored, like her brothers and sisters, so she wouldn't stand out so much. In Prairie City, she always had to wear a bonnet pulled close about her face, so no one would notice and think she was a white girl and maybe cause some trouble.

Sometimes Sass kind of envied her sister's pale, pretty face, but usually she didn't mind her own round, dark chubby face, her big eyes, and tightly braided hair. Once when Jo suggested Sass wear her hair fluffed about her face and decorated with bright bows, Mama just laughed. "You know this child'd lose those ribbons 'fore nightfall, girl. What you thinking, anyway? Your papa earning enough to keep buying peck sacks full of ribbons for this here child's hair?"

Sass wondered if Mama had been like her when she was a girl. Somehow she couldn't see her being as fussy as Jo or as quiet as their older sister, Annie. But Mama was raised a slave with no say-so of her own. "I was property, same's a horse or a cow," Mama had told them many times. "Whatever you told to do, you hop to it, or else."

Sass was sure glad those days of slavery were over. She was glad, too, that they lived out here on the prairies of Kansas where they were free to be whatever they had a wish to be, mostly anyways, if they had, what Papa called "the where-with-all."

As Sass rounded the corner of their two-story, limestone rock house, she saw her father loading their bedding into the wagon. The horses, Sam and Molly, hitched and waiting, stood dozing in the sun. Her brother, Gabriel, always came in from his farm to work on the paper whenever Papa had to be gone, which usually wasn't often. Today, though, Papa had newsprint to pick up off the train in Prairie City, and Mama wanted to buy some yard goods for a couple of new dresses. Her other brother, Jimmy, would help Gabriel until they picked him up on the way out of town. Jimmy liked to help with the paper, but he liked going to Prairie City, more.

Prairie City was the county seat and the end of the line for the railroad. Folks were saying that the railroad was soon going to be built on past Prairie City to Solomon Town and on west. Papa believed the train would bring in both colored and white folks. He believed they could have a town where the races could live together in harmony and peace. But Mama said that was because Papa had never been a slave. "Being born to free parents, he only got about half an idea what white folks do." Her voice, anger-colored, she'd added, "Get white folks in here and right off they gonna go to shoving and a pushing until colored folks back to being washerwomen and white people's grave-diggers and whatever else be the dirty work."

There were already two white families in Solomon Town, and one white girl coming, if Jo knew what she was talking about. The white folks here didn't push and shove and Mama liked them, so it was a little confusing to Sass as to why her mother got so upset over a few more white people moving into Solomon Town.

"We don't be needing no railroad, George," Mama stormed at Papa one day.

"But, Sarah, you want our town to have a library and a bigger church. More people would mean more funds to build them."

"Maybe," she'd answered, "but more'n likely a bunch of whites be moving in, and pretty soon we'd be looking on the outside of a big, tall steepled church and a library shut to black folks."

Sass had heard stories that made the skin under her braids tingle and goose bumps raise up on her arms. Stories about men and women treated worse than dogs, with no dignity or worth at all. Like the colored man shot in the head by a bragging white man who boasted that he could shoot the ear off a "nigger." *And nobody did a thing. Like it didn't matter at all to nobody.*

Those stories scared her. Still, she couldn't help but daydream about a train stopping in Solomon Town, and Papa, proud and happy, as more and more folks moved into their town. In her daydream, though, the folks who got off that train were always colored folks.

She asked Papa if the railroad came to Solomon Town, would they still sometimes go to Prairie City. "Not so often," Papa said, "but probably some times." She hoped so. She liked to stay in the little dugout just outside of Prairie City.

Because it was too far to travel to Prairie City and back in one day, and because there was a law against colored people staying in town past sundown, they stayed nights at the dugout and started for home the next morning. In clear weather, Sass loved to sleep out under the stars, but on rainy, stormy nights she stayed in the dugout with Mama and her sisters, Jo and Annie. Whether clear or stormy,

Papa and Jimmy slept under the wagon. Sometimes there'd be other families, the men sleeping under their wagons, the women, children, and girls, if it was raining or the air chilly, all crowded into the dugout.

Sass loved it when, on pleasant evenings, everyone sat around talking until bedtime. In the gathering darkness, shadows cast by the glow of a lantern or the flickering firelight lent an air of mystery to the night.

When the train did come to Solomon Town, Papa said they might ride it back to Kentucky and visit some of his relatives and maybe even Mama's sister. Mama held out little hope that her sister would still be there, if they ever did get back to Kentucky.

"She being older than me, she likely dead, or moved on elsewhere," she said. "Maybe sold away before Emancipation come. Us not reading or writing weren't no way we gonna know."

Papa had offered to teach Mama to read and write, but she insisted she was too old, and any extra time he might have would be best spent on their children.

Several times when there was no teacher for the school, Papa spent the day teaching in the schoolhouse and nights at his newspaper office getting out the paper by lamplight. Sass thought of the white girl Jo said was coming to Solomon Town and wondered if she would be going to their school.

Walking up to Sam and Molly, Sass stood between the horses' heads and rubbed each broad, brown forehead. "Jo says a white girl's coming to Solomon Town." She peered around Molly's head at her father. "Says she's Mr. Goodwin's niece."

"That's right." Papa gave her a smile. The brim of his hat shadowed his face, so his eyes, lightened to gray by a mingling of white ancestors, looked as dark as hers.

She ran her hand along the velvety softness of Molly's muzzle. "I wonder if she'll be nice, like him and Mrs. Goodwin."

"Why, I imagine so," Papa said. He turned and took the baskets that Mama and Annie and Jo had brought out of the house and set them in the wagon. "I guess we're all ready to go," he said, smiling.

As Sam and Molly pulled the wagon through the main street of Solomon Town, Mama glanced out toward the prairie. "There's Miss Julia," she said.

"Coming to talk to Miss Reed's hats," Annie said.

Sass, sitting on the backseat behind Mama and Papa and sandwiched in between her sisters, Jo and twenty-year-old Annie, turned her head to watch the old woman hobble across the prairie, her stout walking stick jabbing the ground with every step, her cape fluttering about her like the wings of a big black bird.

Every morning the old woman came into town to visit Miss Reed's millinery store, veering out into the street and around Mr. Mar's bank and Mr. Goodwin's mercantile. "Like they poison," Mama said, "because they's white folks."

At Miss Reed's millinery store, Miss Julia always stood in front of the display stands that Miss Reed used to show off her hats and talked away as if the hats were on the heads of real live women.

Miss Reed had told everyone about Miss Julia. "Don't never catch what she sayin', but it fair gives the chills to see her a talkin', her old head a-bobbin' up and down. Sure do sound like she conjurin' up a spell. It sure do."

Sass thought it was odd that Miss Julia never wore a hat herself, but always the same ragged green and black patterned head-rag twisted about her frizzled gray hair.

Miss Julia lived in a little sod house a half-mile from town. Her neighbors, the Bensons, took care of her, bringing her food and keeping a coal oil can filled for her to use in her lamps. Somehow the Bensons kept her from knowing it all came from Mr. Goodwin's store, otherwise she'd probably dump it all out the door, the way she hated white folks.

Mr. Goodwin was sweeping the steps and the boardwalk in front of his store as they passed by. He raised a hand in greeting and Papa called out a cheerful "Good morning, Caleb."

"*Miss Julia's coming,*" Sass wanted to laughingly shout at Mr. Goodwin, "*You better get inside before she wings you with her evil eye.*" Everyone, but Miss Julia, liked Mr. Goodwin and his wife and the other white folks, Mr. and Mrs. Mars, the banker and his wife. It was said they caused quite a stir when they first arrived, and folks surely did wonder why they'd come to live in a colored town. But now no one paid them any mind, except Miss Julia.

Sass' parents had come out from Kentucky a year before she was born. Gabriel, now grown up, had taken a homestead five miles out on the prairie, and last year, Papa and Jimmy helped him put up a sod house for his new wife. Gabriel often helped Papa in the newspaper office, but he was a farmer at heart. He and Cora were expecting a baby in the middle of winter. Gabriel, fifteen-year-old Jimmy, and her sisters, Annie and Jo, were all born in Kentucky. Sass had been born in the dugout they'd lived in, until last year when Papa had hired some men to build their big, two-story house of limestone rock. The dugout now made a fine barn for Sam and Molly.

As they traveled along the road toward Prairie City, the wagon's wheels rumbling over the road and the horses' hooves clip-clopping along, Sass gazed out across the flat, open land, always watching for deer or fox, the small prairie dog, or some other animal.

They stopped to eat at midday in their usual place beside a hill of limestone rock where a few trees grew along a stream bank providing shade. Here, Mama still reminded Sass how to act in Prairie City.

"Remember," she said, "you don't look white folks in the eyes, and you step clear down in the street if they's coming towards you. Don't go to opening your mouth less'n you're spoken to, and don't be putting your fingers on nothing that's setting in a store to be for sale."

Sass, who could repeat her warnings word for word, heard a squirrel chatter and looked up to see one jump from a tree limb. "Evangeline!" Her mother's use of her real name and the sharp edge to her voice made Sass's cheeks burn with embarrassment.

"Sorry, Mama," she murmured.

Prairie City had grown since their last visit. They noted a new store among the ones already on the main street, and carpenters were hard at work on another new building, the sounds of their hammering and sawing a part of the noise of the bustling streets. Papa noted that a new addition had been added on to the Allyson Hotel. "It's the railroad that's making this town prosper," he said. "Just what we'll have when it comes to Solomon Town."

Papa drove the team directly to the train station to pick up his newsprint. Sass was disappointed not to see a train setting by the station or coming down the long line of tracks. Her disappointment was soon forgotten, however, when Papa dropped them off in front of Mr. Jenkins' Mercantile, and he and Jimmy went on to the livery stable. With hands clasped tightly behind her back, Sass gazed at all the wonderful things on the shelves in Mr. Jenkin's store—so much more than in Mr. Goodwin's mercantile back in Solomon Town. Annie and Jo enjoyed looking too, but Mama, as usual, acted nervous, as she bought her yard goods. Sass knew she was always afraid when they were in town—afraid some white person would accuse them of stealing or something.

In the late afternoon, their trading done, Papa drove them around to the alley behind the Allyson Hotel for supper. He pulled Sam and Molly up a few feet from the back door and, jumping down, went over and knocked. He took off his hat when the blond woman opened the door.

"What do you want?" she demanded, her gaze flickering past Papa and up at them sitting in the wagon, and then back again to Papa's face.

"Could we get supper for six, ma'am?" Papa asked, his fingers turning his hat brim around and around.

"Beans and cornbread?"

"Ham, too, if you please, ma'am. We have the money."

"All right. Wait." The door shut in Papa's face.

He came back to the wagon and stood leaning against it, his back to Mama, his eyes on the door. Mama put a hand down on his shoulder.

They ate in the wagon. Afterwards, Papa set their empty plates back by the door.

The sun was a huge orange ball on the edge of the prairie when they arrived at the dugout. The Bensons came a few minutes later, and they spent a pleasant evening visiting.

At bedtime, Sass spread her blanket just outside the entrance to the dugout. Lying on her back, hands behind her head, she gazed up at the stars in the black velvet sky and listened to the muted sounds of the night. She heard a coyote cry and the distant hoot of an owl. She yawned and was soon asleep. In her dreams, a white girl rode the train into Solomon Town.

~ Chapter Three ~

MAGGIE ROSE

Sunlight filtered through the leaves of the giant oaks and danced across the rows of Goodwin tombstones. Maggie Rose glanced at Grandmother's grave, still a mound of raw earth and as yet, unmarked.

She knelt before her parents' stone and wished she'd thought of bringing flowers for this final goodbye. *In God's Care* was engraved above their names and an unexpected flash of anger made her forget the soreness of her ragged fingernails. She bit down and pain and anger brought tears to blur her vision.

In God's Care? How caring could a god be who took your mother the minute you were born? And while you were still just a little girl, took the father who loved and adored you? How caring of a god could he be to leave a six-year-old with an old, ugly-tempered grandmother and then, take even her away before the child was grown up enough to be on her own? Now she had to go to a place called Kansas—to she knew not what—and live with an uncle she'd never seen.

Despair weakened her burst of anger, and she dropped to her knees at the foot of the graves and let the tears fall in a scalding flow. When her tears were spent, she became conscious of Mr. Foxworth, Grandmother's lawyer, who waited at the foot of the hill, his horse and buggy pulled up under the shade of a tree. Wiping her eyes and nose with the hem of her skirt, she got to her feet. "Well," she said aloud, "whatever's going to happen, will happen."

She drew herself up taller, straighter, and lifted her chin. "Goodbye, Mother. Goodbye, Father. I'll do the best I can." Then she turned away and started down the hill to where Mr. Foxworth waited.

Tomorrow she and Hattie would climb aboard the train bound for Kansas. Hattie's bag and her own small trunk were packed and ready. She supposed Mr. Foxworth had told Hattie she would have to move upstairs and sleep in Aunt Susan's old room and, on Sundays, when she went to visit her friends, stay only a few hours. Anyway, that's how it turned out, and Maggie Rose was grateful, for when she was alone, the house loomed large and frighteningly empty. Hattie was also going with her to Kansas.

"Since Mr. Caleb be providin' my passage back, I'll go 'long," Hattie had said in her usual quiet voice. The wave of relief that washed over her at Hattie's words had left Maggie Rose weak and trembling, for she had been sick with fear over the prospect of traveling that long, long way alone.

Mr. Foxworth drove them to the train station through a light drizzle of rain. As they were leaving the house, he'd given Maggie Rose a round gold watch to pin to the bodice of her dress and a purse of traveling money. Both, he told her, were an advance against the sale of her grandmother's property. "Hang onto that purse, now. There's liable to be thieves and charlatans riding the train with you."

It scared her to be in charge of the money, and she wished Hattie wasn't colored so he'd have given the purse to her.

At the train station, Mr. Foxworth stepped up to a man wearing a railroad uniform and said, "This colored girl is to sit with Miss Goodwin, as she will be seeing to her care all the way to Kansas."

The man nodded, and as Mr. Foxworth stepped aside, he smiled and offered his hand to help her up into the train. She looked back to be sure Hattie was following and saw the man's smile disappear and his hand drop to his side as Hattie stepped forward. Maggie Rose looked at Hattie's face, but the colored woman's expression never changed as she stepped up, unaided, into the train.

Train travel, Maggie Rose soon found out, was not all that pleasant. The noise level was constant, with the chugging of the engine and the varied voices of the passengers. The smells of stale cigar smoke, sweating bodies, and a kind of musty sourness she couldn't place was nearly overpowering, until finally, she became used to it.

The train stopped along the way to take on more passengers and let others off. Each time a new man climbed aboard, Maggie Rose worried that he might be a thief or a charlatan, and she'd clutch the purse tighter.

Sometimes, the train stayed long enough to let the passengers get off and get a bite to eat. Some places, Hattie was allowed to eat in the kitchen, but some refused to serve her at all. Those times, Maggie Rose brought the colored woman a sandwich, which Hattie ate standing outside behind the building.

Through the long nights, they slept sitting up on the moving train, dozing and waking and dozing again. They changed trains somewhere, a brief stopover early one morning. Maggie Rose thought it was someplace in Maryland, but all she cared was that she'd heard someone say that now they were headed westward, and that gave her hope. But there were still miles to go and, by the time the train had crossed into Missouri, she thought she would never ever be rested again.

Finally, they crossed the Missouri River and entered Kansas, but there was still a long way to go, for Solomon Town, Mr. Foxworth had told her, was located in the middle of the state.

As the hours passed, the rolling hills of eastern Kansas flattened into a great expanse of land, where tall grasses, sprinkled generously with colorful flowers, flowed like water in the wind. The only breaks in the vast skyline were small hills, with an outcropping of a yellowish white rock, and the few trees that grew along the watersheds.

The proprietor of the Allyson Hotel met them at the Prairie City depot. Taking Maggie Rose's small trunk, he ushered them down an alley and into the hotel by the back door. There, a woman waited and hurried them up the back stairs to a room on the second floor.

Closing the door, she leaned against it and said to Maggie Rose, "Your uncle paid for you and your...umm," she hesitated then added, "girl to stay here, tonight. The mail stage to Solomon Town goes at eight o'clock in the mornin'. If you're of a mind to go out and look around tonight, there ain't no law saying you can't. But," she jerked her head toward Hattie, "she'd better stay in this room 'til the stage gets here in the morning. Do I make myself clear?"

Maggie Rose nodded. "What about our supper?"

"I'll bring it up to you at six. Breakfast's at seven." She turned to leave and then looked back again at Maggie Rose. "'Member now, she's not to go out. We got a sundown law here in this town. Can't no coloreds stay the night. Soon's the sun sets, they got to be out of town. Your uncle, he got a special permit for her. We'll fumigate the room soon's you leave, but if she's seen, folks'll not be likin' it at all."

"All right." Maggie Rose hardly heard what the woman was saying. She was so tired. She just wanted her to go away. But the woman went on about having two of everything—pitchers of water, washbasins, towels, and chamber pots. Maggie Rose wanted only to lie down on the bed, big enough for two people. She was glad there was a cot for Hattie, so she wouldn't have to sit up all night.

As the door closed behind the woman, Hattie said, "Saw a wagon with some colored folks. I imagine they gettin' on out of town 'cause of the law."

Maggie Rose frowned. "What law?"

"The sundown law, the missus just told us about. 'Member?"

Maggie Rose shook her head and, sinking down on the bed, was soon asleep.

At six o'clock, as she'd promised, the woman brought their supper. Maggie Rose was almost too tired to eat and afterwards fell asleep again.

She woke to a splash of sun across her bed and Hattie shaking her shoulder. "It be near seven, Miss. She be bringin' breakfast soon."

The woman brought them two plates of biscuits and gravy, and a few minutes before eight, she came back to escort them downstairs. Again they used the back door. The woman led them around the building to where the mail stage, hitched to four brown mules, waited at the front of the hotel.

"Your uncle provided a bite for midday," the woman said as she thrust a small package, wrapped in brown paper and tied with a string, into Maggie Rose's hands. Then she turned on her heel and went back inside the hotel.

The driver was a cheerful man with twinkling brown eyes and a bushy brown mustache. There were no other passengers, and they rode in silence, the driver's cheery voice calling out now and then to the mules.

By the watch Maggie Rose had pinned to her bodice, it was 5:00 p.m. when the driver called out, "Solomon Town just ahead!"

Maggie Rose had expected a bigger town, but what surprised her more as the driver drove his mules down through what appeared to be the main street of town, the only people about were colored. Panic clutched at her and she swung around, searching the street for a white face. At a chuckle from Hattie, she looked up at the usually somber faced woman. "Sure didn't 'spect to find this many coloreds 'round here," Hattie said.

Fear rose up, drying Maggie Rose's mouth. She licked her lips and swallowed. What? *Was this town full of colored people?*

"Coming, Miss?" The stage had stopped, and the driver had the door open and was holding out his hand. In a daze she stood up, and as the man helped her step down on to the ground, she saw they were in front of a building—a post office, the sign said. Dark eyes looked at her out of a crowd of dark faces. She glanced wildly about, and suddenly, a white face and a head of brown hair came into her range of vision. Uncle Caleb? She nearly collapsed with relief.

"Maggie Rose!" Uncle Caleb was holding her hands and smiling down at her. "My goodness! Mother never told me you were a young lady. I guess I was expecting a child."

He released her hand and, still smiling, turned to greet Hattie and introduce her to a colored woman standing nearby. "This is Mrs. Martin," he said. "Our accommodations are quite small and cramped, so she is offering her home to you. She has a fine, big stone house, very spacious. I'm sure you will be most comfortable there."

Mrs. Martin, a small, slender woman in a pink flowered dress, smiled at Hattie. Two younger women stood beside her. One of the women was definitely colored, but the other one looked white. A darker-skinned girl came up beside them—a girl near her own age, Maggie Rose thought. This girl had braided hair in rows and a round, dark face with large black eyes that looked steadily into hers, before Maggie Rose looked away.

Mrs. Martin introduced Hattie to the three, calling them daughters. Curious about the dark girl, Maggie Rose listened only for her name. Sass is certainly an odd name, she thought.

Uncle Caleb helped her up into a big, high wagon hitched to two gray mules he called Big Boy and Muley. As they set off down a road leading across the flat prairie land, she looked back. A large stone house rose above the prairie, not far from the street they had just come down in the mail coach. "That's the Martin home where Hattie will stay while she's here," Uncle Caleb said. She smiled. Then Uncle Caleb's house had to be much, much bigger.

He probably could have kept Hattie, but didn't want to have coloreds in his house, except for hired help. She wondered about Aunt Olivia. Did she like living in a town with so many coloreds? Then a sudden horrifying thought struck her. *Aunt Olivia? Was she white or colored?*

They were out on the prairie now away from the town, and she saw that a few houses scattered across the land appeared to be made of grass—at least grass grew on the roofs, some of it so tall it waved in the wind. As they approached a long, low building that looked like it was made out of squares of dirt, stacked together like bricks, Uncle Caleb said, "Well this is home, Maggie Rose." Her eyes flew to the roofline, but instead of grass, she was relieved to see that the house was roofed with boards, as a house ought to be.

Uncle Caleb brought the mules to a stop in front of the dirt house and, jumping down, helped Maggie Rose out of the wagon. She stood before a wide plank door that suddenly opened and a woman with fair hair and blue eyes stepped out of the house, a baby in her arms. Two little boys, both fair-haired and blue-eyed, peered at her from around the woman's skirts.

"Hello, Maggie Rose." Aunt Olivia's smile was warm. "Welcome to our home and into our family."

For a moment Maggie Rose couldn't answer, so relieved was she that Aunt Olivia was white. "H…Hello," she finally managed.

The little baby in Aunt Olivia's arms cooed and clapped her chubby little hands together. She, too, had flaxen hair and blue eyes.

Aunt Olivia laughed. "Sally Ann welcomes you as well, Maggie Rose." She half turned to the little boys hiding behind her skirts. "This is Robert and Benjamin. Can you say 'Hello' to Maggie Rose?" she asked. The little boys drew back out of sight behind her skirts, and again their mother laughed.

"Please do come on in." She stood to one side, the little boys taking small sideways steps to stay behind her. With a weak-feeling smile, Maggie Rose stepped past them into the house.

The first impression Maggie Rose had of the house was that it was cool, a welcome relief from the heat and the glaring sun. *But it was a dirt house! How could they live in a dirt house?* She had to admit, though, it looked clean and pleasant. The floor was made of wide wooden planks, and several colorful rag rugs were scattered about. The squares of sod inside the house had been white-washed and that, she supposed, brightened the room. Blue-checked curtains decorated the two small windows, and a blue-patterned oilcloth covered the table. The room seemed to be part kitchen and part sitting room.

"First of all, " Aunt Olivia said, "I'll show you where you'll sleep." She pulled aside a heavy curtain, and Maggie Rose stepped into a room just big enough for two beds and a small dresser. The beds were covered with colorful, pieced quilts and Aunt Olivia gestured toward one. "This will be yours. The boys will share the other."

As she backed out and Aunt Olivia let the curtain fall back into place, Maggie Rose saw another curtained off room. "That's your Uncle Caleb's and mine," Aunt Olivia said. "Sally Ann sleeps in our room."

So she had to sleep with the little boys. Well, at least she wouldn't have the baby in there, too. She thought of Hattie staying in the nice big house of stone. Probably she had her own room and all the privacy she wanted. *Dear Heavens, wouldn't Grandmother have a fit if she could see where her son lived? Not just in a dirt house, but in a town full of coloreds.* She bit her lip to hold back a rise of hysterical laughter. *Why, if Grandmother knew this, she'd be spinning like a top in her grave.*

~ *Chapter Four* ~

SASS

Sass knew it wouldn't take her mama long to have Miss Hattie Smith settled in and feeling right at home. And, sure enough, by the time they'd sit down to supper, she'd become just plain Hattie, laughing over Papa's stories and exclaiming over Mama's cooking.

Gabriel and Cora had come for supper, too, and Hattie and Cora had hit it off right from the start. Mama said later that although Hattie was a good twenty years the older, they had the same quiet ways about them and a true passion for growing things, especially flowers. As soon as Gabriel moved Cora into their sod house, Cora had hurried to plant their vegetable garden, so she could get started on a flower garden.

Later that summer, as she stood admiring Cora's flowers, Mama said, "Don't know how you grow such lovely flowers, child, with these terrible, hot Kansas winds bent on drying the ground fast as a body puts water to it."

Cora had beamed with pride at Mama's praise.

Now Hattie, arranging, in a clear glass pitcher, the white daisies and blue bachelor buttons Cora had brought from her garden to grace the dinner table, said, "I did so love growin' flowers. Some friends let me plant some at their house, since I had no place of my own, and Pearl

Goodwin wasn't likely to allow it at her house, even if I was to ask." A small smile touched her dark eyes. "She was close about spendin' both cash money and my time. Wasn't one given to seein' beauty, either, even if it got stuck right up in her old white face."

They talked of flowers for a while and then other things, laughing and sharing, until Sass thought it was almost like Christmas or the Celebration. By the time they had all pushed back from the table, Papa and Gabriel groaning and patting full stomachs, Hattie might well have been one of the family. Papa always said Mama had the gift for making folks feel comfortable, and her cooking was like manna from heaven.

"No one cooks better'n our mama," Gabriel said, his dark eyes warm on Mama's face. Then shifting his gaze to Cora's, he added, "But Cora's learning. Aren't you, dear?"

Cora's big eyes, soft as butter on Gabriel, sparkled with a sudden grin as she turned to Mama. "That boy of yours sure do gobble up my sweet custard, though. He got no complaint about that. But I sure do wish I could make light bread good as yours, Mama."

"Don't you be worryin' your sweet head over that, honey-girl," Mama said, "Your flowers be pleasin' as my cookin'. And, Lord, girl, I've been a-workin' at cookin' since going on to ten years old."

"Younger than Sass," Papa said.

A faraway look came over Mama's face and swept the softness from her eyes. "I came squallin' into this world down in the slave quarters on the Briggs plantation in Mississippi," she began. "Mama say I don't act happy at all about gettin' born." Her eyes crinkled and a smile touched her lips. "Mama say she sure do understand, but it be too late now."

They all knew Mama's story, but she would tell it now for Hattie. "Wasn't 'til I was near seventeen that I got sold off—my sister, Flora, and me. We go to Kentucky, ridin' in a wagon in chains along with a couple of other colored folks." She paused and smiled at Papa. "And there, I meets you."

She turned her attention from Papa's smiling face, back to Hattie and went on with her story. "George and his daddy, they be free coloreds and they save up to buy my freedom."

"Nine hundred dollars," Sass said. It never failed to touch her with awe that her papa loved her mama enough for him and his papa to pay that huge sum of money.

Mama smiled, nodding at Sass, and went on with her story of how she had been taken at ten years of age from the cotton fields to work in the kitchens of the big houses, first in Mississippi and then in Kentucky.

"I bet you made good mud pies when you were little," Sass said, smiling at her mother. "Remember that time when I was little and you said my mud pies lookin' so good, I was surely goin' to be a real cook someday."

Mama chuckled. "I remember. But just talkin' to please you, honey-girl. You just playin' in the mud 'cause it be outdoors. If I was to make you bring that dirt and water inside, pretty quick you'd be back outside doin' somethin' else." Her face sobered. "Myself, can't remember makin' mud pies. Had plenty of dirt, though. Recall sittin' in it out in the cotton fields waitin' on Mama, 'til I get big enough to pick 'long side her. Pickin' cotton's an awful job, but I hated leavin' Mama when I got taken up to the big house. In both places, cotton fields or the big house, there don't be no playin' time once you big enough to work."

Sass ducked her head, feeling the heat of shame rush to her face. *How could she so easily forget how difficult her mother's life had been in those slave years?*

Papa's hand found Sass's under the table and gave it a squeeze. "I was lucky enough to be born to free parents," he said, smiling at Mama before turning to Hattie. "My father was a tailor and was well thought of in our community. My mother had quite an education for a colored girl. She was a born teacher with only me to teach. I used to hide when it was lesson time and I wanted to stay outdoors and play." His gray eyes warmed with his smile, then sobered as he looked at Hattie. "I would gather life wasn't so easy for you as a child."

"No, sir, it wasn't. I was born and raised up in Georgia. The master sold me off when I just past seven years old." Hattie's hand went to her throat and shadows seemed to fill the hollow planes of her face. She swallowed, and her hand dropped back to her lap. "Never saw my mama ever again."

Sass knew Hattie had tried to push past the pain of that memory—knew she had tried to will her words to come out steady and calm. But the raw, ragged edge of grief still clung to them—unshakeable, even after all those years. In her mind's eye, Sass could see the little girl being pulled away, her arms held out to her mama, as she cried and screamed in grief and fear. With a little jolt of her heart, she realized there were some hurts so deep they never entirely went away. She hung her head and lowered her eyelashes to hide the sudden gathering of tears.

"A man's hands lift me up on to the slave block," Hattie continued. "'*Don't you cry,*' he warned. So I don't dare, though I want to bad." She took a drink from her water glass and set it back on the table, her hand turning it slowly, her eyes on the glass. When she spoke again, her voice sounded firmer, stronger. "Some folks bought me for their two girls 'bout my same age, and I grew up with them. When Emancipation come, I need a last name, so I take theirs." She shrugged. "It's good as any other, I s'pose." A sudden grin flashed across her face. "Better'n takin' Pearl Goodwin's anyway."

"Most slave folks took the name of their former masters," Papa said. "Sarah, here," he smiled at Mama, "just took mine. And I was one proud man to be able to give it to her."

Sass caught the quick look of affection that passed between her parents and felt a warm glow of contentment.

"I learned to read and write along with those girls," Hattie went on with her story. "They knew I wasn't to learn, but they never did give much mind to what was s'pose to be. They had me speakin' poems and readin' aloud, 'til their daddy catch me. He set me in a dark, little room for a night and a day. Got to seeing things weren't there and I sure be awful scared. Doubt if the girls even scolded. It don't stop them none, either. They soon playin' like before, but I was jumpy as a frog and so plain scared of gettin' caught, I don't learn no more. When the girls growed up and the oldest one married, I got sent to her home with the other slaves their daddy give her for a weddin' present. A year passed and she got a fever and die. Her husband sold me off to the Goodwins."

Not a word was spoken as Hattie told her story. Like her, Sass noted that her brothers and sisters often looked down at their hands or stirred uncomfortably in their chairs. Mama kept nodding and murmuring some deep feeling sound in her throat, and Papa's gray eyes rarely left Hattie's face. When Hattie told of being sold away from her mama, Cora's eyes brimmed with tears, and her hands closed around her stomach where her unborn child was beginning to show.

"I turn twenty years old when Emancipation come," Hattie was saying. "Free, but don't feel like free. Just scared... no family... just me by myself, and everywhere coloreds, same as me, leavin' plantations, and places they don't have to stomach no more, and tryin' hard to find work, and work not easy to find." She paused, and a distant look shadowed her eyes.

"So you stayed on with Pearl Goodwin," Papa said.

Hattie nodded. "Her husband was dead, and she had those three children, though all near grown. Besides Caleb here, there was Susan and Edward. Pearl Goodwin shut her eyes and ears to the girl, Susan, when she married. Never again spoke her name. Mr. Edward, Miss Maggie Rose's daddy, died when the girl just six years old. Her mama passed on the night the child was born. Miss Amanda was the sweetest girl. I did so grieve for her. She wasn't more'n sixteen." A shadow flickered across Hattie's face. "Mr. Edward was a good man too. I surely did feel sorry when he died, and that little o' girl got stuck with Pearl Goodwin. I don't care to be speaking ill of the dead, but Pearl Goodwin had a mean soul."

"I understand the Goodwin girl is about Sass' age," Papa said. "Do you think she would accept an offer of friendship from Sass?" Sass looked quickly up at her father. *Friends with that blue-eyed, white girl with hair down to her waist and skin as pale and delicate looking as eggshells? How could they possibly be friends?* No. If the girl took up a friendship with anyone it would be Jo, with her beautiful face and skin like eggs shells too, but the pale brown kind. Jo never got dirty or moved faster than a

35

lady-like walk. No, it was pretty doubtful that Miss White Girl would want to be friends with dark o' outdoors Sass.

"Afraid Miss Maggie Rose is going to be needin' some time," Hattie said. "She's a good girl, but used to the ways of the South where colored people way beneath whites."

"Her uncle doesn't think that way," Papa said.

"No. As I recall, he's a person sees under the surface of things. Always has treated colored folks same as white. All the children tended to lean that way. Miss Susan got married to a man with some colored blood. He was light enough to pass for white, but Pearl Goodwin would've rather seen her daughter dead 'fore marrying up with a man that's got even a drop of colored blood."

"She sounds 'bout like our Miss Julia Hardy," Mama said and then explained to Hattie how Miss Julia hated all white people.

"I s'pect her and Pearl Goodwin got cut from the same cloth," Hattie said and then added with a grin, "I s'pect, though, your Miss Julia's cloth be homespun. Reckon Pearl Goodwin'd die 'fore she'd wear homespun."

They all smiled, and then Hattie began again to speak of the white girl's grandmother. "Pearl Goodwin's husband died of pneumonia in the war. But that wasn't prideful enough for Pearl Goodwin, so she put him to dying bravely on the battlefield, killing colored-loving Yankees. To her, the war got started by us colored folks."

"And how did we do that?" Gabriel asked with a little snort of a laugh.

Hattie smiled at him. "Seems we all got tired of bowin' and grinnin' at our masters, so we goes and gets the North all riled up, so's they'd start the war and kill her husband." Hattie shook her head. "She always made her own truth. Don't matter what other people say. Don't listen anyhow.

Soon, don't no one care to see her, and she dry up tighter and meaner. Maggie Rose bound to have troubles here being raised by Pearl Goodwin."

"Sad for the child," Mama said.

"Well, she has a nice family now." Papa pushed back his chair and got to his feet. "Let's hope for her sake she can see that her grandmother's ideas were wrong."

A cloud shadow darkened the room, and a sudden cool breeze wafted in through the open windows. Papa and Gabriel both went to the door to scan the sky. "It could rain," Gabriel said.

At his words, Jimmy jumped up from his chair and went to look for himself. "Aw," he said, "some of us fellas was gonna get up a ball game this evening."

Mama smiled. "Sure do hate to see your ball game get ruined, son." She looked toward the window. "But my prayers been fixed on rain comin'."

"My fields sure needing it," Gabriel said. He and Papa stepped outside to take up chairs on the porch. Jimmy hurried off to the baseball field he and his friends had made behind the livery stable.

Mama got to her feet and began clearing the table. Sass scraped her plate into the garbage pail and stacked it on top of the others waiting to be washed. With Annie, Jo, Cora, and even Hattie helping Mama, there wasn't really any need for her, she decided. And when her mother looked at her, but didn't say anything, she went out to the porch where Papa and Gabriel were discussing the yearly Emancipation Celebration to be held next weekend.

She sat on the steps awhile and listened to them talk. The stray cat jumped up on her lap, purring. She'd named the big gray Miss Muff when Mama finally relented and let her keep her, as long as she stayed outside. Mama wasn't overly fond of cats.

"Looks like the rain's gone on west of us." Mama, with Hattie and the girls following after her, had stepped out on to the porch and was peering out at the clearing sky.

At Mama's words, a dove began cooing its soft mournful call. It sounded like a dove, but Sass was pretty sure it was her friend, Mary. She gathered Miss Muff up in her arms and stood up, nestling the purring cat up under her chin until she saw her best friend coming across the street and up to the front gate. "Mary's here, Mama," she said. "Can we go for a walk?"

Mama, listening to Papa tell Hattie about the Celebration, nodded. "Just don't go far," she said. "It soon goin' to be dark."

Mary Walker was Sass's age. Her mother was a full-blooded Indian, and it showed in Mary's high cheekbones and in her straight black hair, kept in long braids. Her father, who had died last year of an infection from a cut on his leg, had been colored. After his death, Mary and her mother had moved out of their sod house on the prairie to live with an old couple in a sod house in town. Old Auntie's memory was nearly gone and Old Uncle was too crippled up to get around anymore, so Mary's mother tended to their needs in exchange for a place to live. For cash money, she baked for Mrs. Mars, the banker's wife.

"I saw the white girl when she came in on the stage," Sass said as the girls walked along the dusty street.

"What she like?" Mary asked.

Sass shrugged. "I don't know. But Hattie says she probably going to be one of those thinking she's better than us."

They reached the end of the street where the sod schoolhouse stood shaded by the two tall trees the first

MAGGIE ROSE AND SASS

teacher had brought all the way from Kentucky. This year they'd have a man teacher, an ex-slave whose former owner had branded with an X on the top of his right cheek, close to the eye. The man had come to town in late spring driving an old mule hitched to a rickety wagon. He'd come from somewhere in the deep South with two large boxes of books and the desire to give an education to as many colored children as he possibly could.

"S'pose that white girl gonna go to our school?" Mary dropped down beside Sass under one of the trees everyone still called Miss Johnson's trees.

"I doubt it," Sass said. "Can't think that girl's going to have much to do with us coloreds."

Mary sighed. "She be awful lonely then."

"Well, if that's how she's wanting it," Sass muttered, a dark anger spreading through her. "That's going to be perfectly fine with me."

~ Chapter Five ~

MAGGIE ROSE

"*We're going to a colored celebration?*" Maggie Rose looked up from her plate, a fork full of mashed potatoes halfway to her mouth. Later she would think how fortunate it was that the potatoes weren't in her mouth or she'd have choked on them.

"Of course," Aunt Olivia said smiling. "And we'll have a wonderful time."

Maggie Rose couldn't believe it! Not only did she have to live in a town full of coloreds, but now she was expected to go to one of their celebrations. Celebration of what?

Uncle Caleb found her astonishment amusing, and she couldn't help but feel a little miffed when he laughed at her. "I forgot you were raised by my mother," he said, his brown eyes twinkling. "It sounds strange to you now, but once you get acquainted with the girls your age, you'll enjoy it."

"White girls?" Maggie Rose asked. "That girl at the stage stop, was she white? But why was she with that colored family?"

"No." Uncle Caleb smiled. "She's the Martins' daughter all right, just lighter-skinned than the rest of them. There's just us and Mr. and Mrs. Mars, the banker and his wife." Maggie Rose looked at him questioningly, and he added, "They have no children."

A sense of hopelessness settled over Maggie Rose. She would be as lonely here as she had been back in Georgia. She had hoped to make friends, but all the girls here were colored. She didn't suppose this town, small as it was, had a library, either.

"It'll be nice having you here to help me this year," Aunt Olivia said. She turned her head to warn Bennie, as they called the smallest boy, to stop kicking the table leg, and then looked back again at Maggie Rose. "We'll have a lot of cooking to do for the Celebration."

"I'd love to help you, Aunt Olivia." The thought of helping her aunt do the cooking lifted her spirits a little. "But I'm afraid I won't be much help. Hattie always cooked for us, except on Sundays, and then she left things that were no bother for me to fix."

Aunt Olivia smiled. "Just having two extra hands will help me a lot. especially if this little pumpkin gets to fussing." As she talked, she spooned tiny bits of mashed potatoes into Sally Ann's little rosebud of a mouth and wiped the dribbles off the baby's chin with a corner of her bib. "The Celebration will give you the opportunity to meet the other girls here. I want you to try and make friends. I suppose it seems odd to you now, but when you get to know them, you will find that they are really no different than white girls."

No different than white girls? How ridiculous! Maggie Rose wondered if her Uncle Caleb and Aunt Olivia, although they seemed like nice, normal people, weren't a bit addled in the head. *Of course, colored girls were different than white girls.*

"The Martins' daughter, Sass, is near your age, I believe," Uncle Caleb said. "She has a very nice, respectable family. You would do well to be acquainted with her."

I don't think so. Of course Maggie Rose didn't say the words, only thought them.

In her mind's eye, she saw the girl at the stage stop with the round, dark face and big eyes, black as chunks of coal...sassy eyes, bold as you please, eyes. Probably how she got her name. Well, she might be bold and sassy here in Kansas and get away with it, but in Georgia she wouldn't be looking at a white girl that way. No, ma 'am! What was the matter with these people anyway? Uncle Caleb and Aunt Olivia had to be a little crazy to want to live in a town full of colored people. Without thinking of how rude the question sounded, she blurted out, "Why did you move here to live with these people, anyway?"

"Opportunity, Maggie Rose," Uncle Caleb answered. "That's why most folks settle one place or another. It's why these colored folks came here to Kansas. We all want to better our situations, whoever and wherever we are. It's a common human trait."

"Didn't they care when you and Mr. and Mrs. Mars moved into their town?"

"You're thinking if it were the other way around, colored people moving into a white town, there'd be a whale of a fuss. Right?"

Maggie Rose nodded.

"Well, it didn't happen here. They seemed cordial enough and in many cases even helpful. The Martins in particular." Suddenly Uncle Caleb grinned. "Except for Miss Julia Hardy. She hates all white people. That old girl wouldn't step one foot in my store or in Mr. Mars' bank if her life depended on it. When we started building the store, she shook her walking stick at us and yelled that she was going to burn it down. I think she would have, too, but George Martin got her to calm down."

"Is he that Sass girl's father?" Maggie Rose asked.

"Yes. He's a good man. I'd stake my life on anything he says he'll do. He's good with folks, too. I doubt if anyone else could have calmed Miss Julia down. She's one hateful, old woman. Reminds me of my mother."

"Well, if she's like Grandmother, I don't care to meet her," Maggie Rose said and then ducked her head in embarrassment. *Even if he'd said it, she ought not—not about his mother.*

But Uncle Caleb appeared not to have heard, for he began talking about a railroad coming to Solomon Town and how it would help the community grow. "They're already surveying, so I can't help but think it's going to happen."

"Why wouldn't Prairie City be just as good a place to live?" Maggie Rose asked. "It already has a railroad."

"If we get the railroad, there's no doubt this town will surpass Prairie City. We have the river and several good-sized streams. I can see great potential here. And we'll be in on the beginning...the ground floor. That's where the money is."

The next day, when she was helping Aunt Olivia do the dishes, Maggie Rose asked what foods she planned to take to the Celebration.

"I'll fry up a few chickens and bake a ham. I'll also make a chocolate cake and a few pies. Probably some sliced cucumbers and melons from the garden, and my cornbread specialty."

"How do you make that?" Maggie Rose asked. She'd found that talking helped to keep down the nervous fluttering in her stomach. She was scared to death about going to the Celebration. *What would she do there? Would a girl her own age, a colored girl, try to be friends?* She hoped not. She'd have no idea what to say to a colored girl.

Maggie Rose tried to listen to Aunt Olivia telling her how to make her cornbread dish, but it was hard to pay attention, and she caught only some of the words. "...corn and carrots and potatoes and onions and some parsnips all cooked together... a cream sauce... a cornbread crust. Pickles."

"Pickles in cornbread?" Maggie Rose said, stacking the plates in the cupboard

A twinkle sparkled in Aunt Olivia's blue eyes. "No, dear," she said chuckling. "We'll take the pickles in a separate container." As she picked up the pan of dishwater to throw outside, she turned to Maggie Rose and said softly, "I know you are worried about going to the Celebration, but really, my dear, we all have a grand time. I'm sure you'll enjoy it."

Maggie Rose doubted that she would enjoy the Celebration, but she would put on a good face for Uncle Caleb and Aunt Olivia. Even if they did seem a little mixed up about this colored business, they were awfully good to her, and just as kind as could be. She would not ever want to disappoint them.

She would not find a friend here and that was too bad, but she was used to not having friends. Aunt Olivia thought she should take up with the colored girls here, and maybe that would be all right if she were five or six or so. A lot of small children played with little coloreds, but twelve, unless you were a boy, was way too old for that.

She wished there were books to read, but Solomon Town didn't have a library. Uncle Caleb was sure they'd have one when the railroad came to the town. Uncle Caleb and Aunt Olivia only had the Bible and a health care book. "We had several others," Aunt Olivia told her, "but we gave them to the school."

School! It was the first she'd given thought to school! *Colored children going to school?* Why, she could hardly believe her ears. She had never heard of such a thing. Surely, she wouldn't have to go to school here, with coloreds! When Uncle Caleb saw how well she could read and write and do sums, he'd realize she was too advanced in her studies to go to a colored school. But when she broached the subject, Uncle Caleb did not accept her argument.

"No, Maggie Rose," he said, shaking his head. "School is too important for you to pass up. Besides, it will help you get acquainted. Maybe you won't learn anything new as far as studies go, but you will learn something, I'm sure." He smiled. "Prairie City has just opened a normal school institute, primarily to train teachers, but also to prepare one for college. Next year, we'll see if you can go there."

"A school in Prairie City?" Maggie Rose tried to keep her voice matter-of-fact, but her heart was racing with excitement. *Next year, she could live in Prairie City! And go to a school where they surely had a lot of books! And girls for friends...white girls!* Then reality set in. "But where would I live, Uncle Caleb?"

He smiled. "You would have to board there. As soon as my mother's house sells, I'll have some extra cash and I'll put some aside for that."

At his words, a flutter of hope raised up in her. *So I just have to get through this year... this year of living among coloreds.... Then I can go to school in a town where white people live and I shall have dozens and dozens of girl friends... white girl friends.*

The days before the Celebration were busy ones for Aunt Olivia and for Maggie Rose. She enjoyed helping and the feeling of usefulness the work gave her. Hattie had done everything in Grandmother's house, except their simple Sunday meals. Here, Maggie Rose was constantly busy, either helping with the children, the housework, or the meals. She was learning to cook and to churn butter from the cream skimmed off a pan of milk. She carried water to the garden and had made numerous trips to the small limestone springhouse built up over the well to fetch butter and milk, or to take a dish that needed to be kept cool. Although the house felt cool after being out in the August heat, the even cooler springhouse felt heavenly.

The cellar out back of the house was cool, too, but she didn't like it at all. Dug deep into the ground and covered over with a plank door that took all her strength to open and lay back against the ground, it made her skin crawl to go down the steps into its dank, musty darkness. Aunt Olivia often sent her there for potatoes or other vegetables, or for some of the meat preserved in big stone crocks. Toads and bugs lived in that dimly-lit dirt hole in the ground among the sacks and crocks and jars. She was always afraid she'd step on a toad, or a spider would come down on its web and land in her hair. Then Aunt Olivia told her about the big, dark twister clouds that sometimes came in a roar of wind, dropping from the sky in huge spirals, twisting and turning with a roar like a dozen speeding trains to sweep away and destroy everything in its path. "Then we run to the cellar," Aunt Olivia said.

Maggie Rose shivered. "Do you have them often?" she asked.

"Some years we have several twisters in the area, and some years none."

"Do you close the cellar door then? When we're down there?"

"Why, yes. Of course."

Maggie Rose wasn't sure but what she would rather take her chances with the storm than to endure a closed cellar door.

A few days before the Celebration, Maggie Rose looked over her few dresses and finally, with Aunt Olivia's help, decided on her blue cotton print. The dress was old, the material a little thin and slightly faded, but Aunt Olivia said it was still a pretty dress.

Hattie had let out the seams and lowered the hem as she had done with most of Maggie Rose's other dresses, once muttering under her breath, "*If that old woman don't buy this child some clothes, soon she goin' to be naked as the day she came into this world.*"

Always afterwards, she had noted how the other girls dressed and knew that her clothes were often the shabbiest, but thanks to Hattie, always clean and carefully mended. She wondered how Hattie was getting along in that big, stone house. She supposed she would be at the Celebration, and that Sass girl was certain to be there too.

~ *Chapter Six* ~

SASS

"Looks like we'll have a good day for the Celebration," Papa said, as he came in from outside. "Might turn off hot by afternoon, though."

"Be cooler down on the river," Mama answered with a smile.

Sass thought her Mama looked especially pretty today in her summer dress of pale green.

She was pleased with her own new lilac-colored dress that Annie had sewn from the material purchased on their last trip into Prairie City. Annie had also sewn a new dress for herself and for Jo, but Mama was wearing her dress from several summers ago.

Sass helped load the crocks, jars, and boxes of food into the wagon. Her mouth watered at the smell of chicken still hot from the frying pan, and her eyes admired the swirls of deep, rich, vanilla frosting covering Mama's sweet raisin cake. Everything looked and smelled so good. With all the good food on Celebration Day, Sass always wished her stomach would somehow suddenly hold more.

"There," Mama said, as she surveyed the food now loaded into the back of the wagon. Her hands on her hips, her face beamed with satisfaction. Then she remembered the tablecloths and sent Sass back into the house for them.

As Sass gathered up the red-checkered cloths Mama used for the Celebration, a sweet melodious sound drifted in through the open window. For a moment Sass dismissed it as a meadowlark singing, then she laughed to herself and hurried outside. "Mary's coming, Mama," she said, handing her mother the tablecloths. "Will it be all right if I go now?"

With her mother's consent, Sass ran to meet her friend who was coming up the road. "Girl, you got that near perfect," she said, smiling at Mary. "Still don't see how you do it. I try and try and nothing sounding like a bird ever comes out."

Mary grinned. "Mama says it's my Indian blood, but she hardly even do a good hoot owl and her blood is all Indian."

Sass laughed. "I can even do a hoot owl. I think your mother can, too."

"Maybe," Mary said, her black eyes dancing. "Mama sure do a good wolf, though. Makes shivers on my skin. She say if we was to follow Indian ways, her spirit guide would be the wolf. I guess mine'd be a bird. Maybe the dove… Maybe the meadowlark."

"I wonder what mine would be?" Sass said, and caught herself from looking around for her mother. One thing her mama didn't like was talk about spirits, unless they were Heavenly spirits."

Mary cocked her head, squinting, while she thought. Then she straightened her head and a bright gleam came into her eyes. "The squirrel," she said. "Curious, adventuresome, bright-eyed, quick…"

"I like that." Sass made a sound that Mary said sounded like a squirrel with the bellyache, and the two friends laughcd and walked on toward the river and the Celebration grounds.

Families from the outlying farms were beginning to arrive, and the prairie was dotted with wagons, buggies, and horseback riders coming in from all directions. As they passed those walking to the river, they called out cheery 'Good Mornings' and other greetings, the men tipping their hats.

Sass loved the Celebration, although she knew she couldn't appreciate it half so much as those who'd been freed by the signing of the Emancipation Proclamation as well as those brave folks who had left all they knew to travel to this unknown land. It was fitting that this Celebration was held to commemorate the end of slavery and to honor the early settlers of Solomon Town.

Yesterday, Papa, Gabriel, and Jimmy had joined the other men down at the Celebration grounds, hauling benches from the church and the school house and setting up makeshift tables under the cottonwood trees. The stage and the speaker's platform would be checked over and any repairs made. The outhouses, idle since the last Celebration, were cleaned of cobwebs and mouse droppings, the walls given a fresh coat of whitewash. Two whole hogs had been roasting over open pits since early this morning, and melons were cooling in the river. Everything would be as ready as it could possibly be and even the weather was perfect—not too hot, and no rain in sight.

The Celebration grounds were alive with people when they arrived, the men shaking hands and clapping each other on the shoulder and talking of crops, the weather, and livestock. Mama, in the midst of the women folk whose talk centered on new babies, food, and folks who were ailing, was introducing Hattie.

Sass spied Gabriel and Cora and smiled at the tender way her brother released his wife to the women and turned toward the men. Gabriel had always sort of hovered over Cora anyway, but now that she was carrying their child, he reminded Sass of a moth drawn to a light.

Every colored person in the area attended the Celebration, unless sickness kept them away. Some could make it only for today's festivities and the evening dance; some would come tomorrow for the Sunday services and the noon meal. But most came prepared to stay the entire time. Those who lived in Solomon Town or close around would go home tonight and return in the morning; the others would stay to sleep out under the stars, or in their wagons, or under canvas attached to their wagons in a kind of makeshift tent.

Sass and Mary had just finished helping unload the food from the wagon when Mary poked Sass's arm. "Look," she said with a little jerk of her head. "Look who's here." Sass turned to see the Goodwin wagon being pulled by their two mules. The little boys stood behind their parents, hanging on to the back of the wagon seat. Mrs. Goodwin, in the front seat beside her husband, held the baby. Sitting on the floor of the wagon bed among the baskets, jars, and crocks of food was the white girl, Maggie Rose.

As Caleb Goodwin reined in the mules, the two girls stepped back behind a black buggy where they could watch, unobserved. Caleb Goodwin and the little boys jumped to the ground, and Mr. Goodwin took the baby in one arm and held out a hand to help his wife step down. The white girl, Maggie Rose, just sat there acting like her skirts were nailed to the bottom of the wagon bed.

"Probably thinking, no way she going to mix with us colored folks. Probably thinking our color will rub right off on to her," Sass muttered.

"Don't think we ought to be a spyin'," Mary whispered, plucking at Sass's sleeve. "Let's go."

Sass ignored her. "I bet Miss White Girl's not getting out of that wagon until she has to. Hattie says she was raised to think we are all beneath her."

"She look plain scared to me," Mary said. "Most likely it scare us, too, if we was to be amongst a whole bunch of white people."

Mary's words gave Sass a start. She hadn't thought of that. *The girl probably was scared. Maybe after the noon feed she'd feel more comfortable about being around colored people, and maybe they should go talk to her and see if she'd want to walk around with them.*

~ *Chapter Seven* ~

MAGGIE ROSE

Maggie Rose shivered. She had never before seen such a huge crowd of colored people, and as Uncle Caleb helped her down from the wagon, she wished again that she could have stayed back at the soddy. Her heart was beating like a drum, and her legs felt weak as cooked noodles.

"Will you hold Sally Ann for me?" Aunt Olivia held the little girl out for Maggie Rose to take. "I'll help Uncle Caleb unload the food."

Nestling her face against the baby's soft hair, Maggie Rose watched as more wagons and buggies pulled up, filled with even more colored people, and her trembling arms tightened around Sally Ann until the little girl pulled back, protesting. "Sorry," she whispered.

Aunt Olivia, lifting a gallon jug of lemonade from the back of the wagon, looked back over her shoulder. Her eyes, shifting from her baby to Maggie Rose's face, softened with understanding. "Don't worry," she mouthed. "You'll enjoy it."

Aunt Olivia might think so, but Maggie Rose wasn't so sure. *There were so many people. Colored people...What were they doing in the midst of this... this colored celebration? Shouldn't they have stayed home?* Her hands closed in a fist behind the baby and she clenched her teeth—the need to bite on her ragged fingernails desperately overwhelming. She shifted the baby to one side so she'd have a free hand. Raising her hand to chew along the edge of a thumbnail, her eyes caught sight of the small gold ring on her finger. She drew the hand back and bit down on her bottom lip instead.

This morning she had been sitting on her bed, combing out the tangled ends of her hair, when Aunt Olivia's voice behind the curtain that separated her and the boys' bedroom from the main room, called for permission to enter. Aunt Olivia, unlike Grandmother, never intruded on her privacy.

"I want you to wear this ring of my mother's," Aunt Olivia said, sitting down on the edge of Maggie Rose's bed and taking the gold ring out of the folds of a white, lace-edged handkerchief. "Someday, when Sally Ann is older, I'd like for her to have it, but for now, it would please me if you would wear it."

"Shouldn't you be wearing it?" Maggie Rose asked.

Aunt Olivia smiled. "My mother was a smaller woman than I am. My fingers are much too large."

Aunt Olivia had slipped the ring on Maggie Rose's finger and, still holding her hands, had leaned forward and kissed her cheek. "You're a lovely girl, Maggie Rose," she'd said. "We are so happy to have you as a part of our family."

Those words of kindness had been too much for Maggie Rose. Sobbing she had leaned into her aunt's arms and let some of the bitter loneliness she'd carried so long flow out in a wash of tears. Later, looking at the ring her aunt had entrusted to her—a ring that had to be so precious to Aunt Olivia—she vowed to stop biting her fingernails. She would make her hands worthy of this small gold ring, set with a purple stone.

When the wagon was unloaded, Uncle Caleb turned the mules around and headed them back home, where he'd turn them out to graze and walk back. A tall colored boy, flanked by two smaller versions of himself, with wide grins and sparkling black eyes, came up to ask Aunt Olivia if he could take Robbie and Bennie down to the river to play with his little brothers. "I'll watch 'em real close, Missus," he said.

Aunt Olivia gave her permission, reminding the boys that they must obey the tall boy she called Joseph, and then she reminded the boy himself to keep the little boys in the shallow part of the river.

Maggie Rose carried Sally Ann and followed along beside her aunt to an area near a stage-like structure mounted with a speaker's stand. In front of the stage, benches, chairs, stools, and colorful blankets were spread out on the ground, provided seating for the large crowd of all ages. As they walked among the colored people, Aunt Olivia introduced Maggie Rose as their niece from Georgia, but to Maggie Rose not a face or a name could be recalled from one introduction to the next. *How strange being introduced to coloreds, just like they were white people.*

Aunt Olivia unfolded the dark-green blanket, she carried, and spread it out on a bare patch of ground next to a faded-blue blanket, where a black woman sat with three little ones around her. Chatting companionably with the colored woman, Aunt Olivia sat down and raised her arms up to take Sally Ann. As soon as Maggie Rose sat down, Aunt Olivia sat the baby between them.

Maggie Rose felt calmer now. Her earlier moments of panic had faded. Sitting down, she didn't feel so of out of place, so exposed to all those dark, dark eyes.

A few minutes after they sat down, a light-skinned colored man, Aunt Olivia said was Mr. Martin, walked up to the speaker's stand. Two white men, one short and plump, the other tall and gangly, walked behind him. "The tall fellow is Mr. Mars, the banker," Aunt Olivia told her. "That short fellow is running for the state senate in Topeka. He's here looking for our men's votes. Of course," she added, a little twinkle coming into her eyes, "he caters to us women, too, even though we can't vote, for he knows we influence our husbands and fathers. This," she added, her hand smoothing Sally Ann's silky, fine baby hair and grinning at Maggie Rose, "is the dull part of the Celebration. But you'll love the rest, especially the music."

Aunt Olivia was right about the speaker, Maggie Rose thought, and as the man droned on and on, she closed her mind to his voice and let her gaze wander around the Celebration grounds. She saw that girl, Sass, and another girl with long, black braids walking side by side. As she watched, she saw them lean in toward each other as if whispering, break apart with a giggle, and walk on.

A stab of envy was quickly replaced with anger. Here were two colored girls acting like white girls, and she, a white girl, sat here feeling like an outcast. *It wasn't fair! No, it wasn't fair at all.* With a sigh, she looked down at Sally Ann asleep on her side, a thumb in her mouth, and wished she could be like her, like a baby, who saw no difference between white and colored people.

When at last the speaker had finished and had left in his small, black buggy, Maggie Rose saw that Aunt Olivia had been right about the music, and listening, she forgot her loneliness.

A colored woman sat at a pump organ. "The organ belongs to Mrs. Mars," Aunt Olivia told her, nodding toward a redheaded woman who stood on the sidelines beside her tall, leggy husband. "She loans it for the Celebration for Clara Ruggles to play. Mrs. Mars taught her to play when she found that Clara had such a wonderful ear for music."

The musical program started off with a small band of colored men playing various instruments, accompanied by the woman on the organ. The men played drums, a banjo and a fiddle, and what Aunt Olivia called a 'wood flute'. Between the numbers by the band, there were solos and duets and various groups of singers, their voices blending in harmony. Best of all, Maggie Rose liked the last performers, four older women whose songs seemed to cast a spell over the crowd. The women clapped as they sang, and their bodies swayed in graceful motion, so their movements and voices blended into a fascinating, beautiful rhythm of sight and sound. Often they shouted words, echoed by the crowd, much of whom were standing now, swaying and stepping with the music.

Following the musical performances, the women put food out on the long tables set up in the shade of two of the largest trees. A tall black man, the Methodist preacher, Aunt Olivia had told her, asked the blessing—a litany of shouted praises.

They ate sitting on the blanket, Uncle Caleb cross-legged with his plate balanced on his lap. Sally Ann lay sleeping between her mother and Maggie Rose. Robbie and Bennie, their pantslegs wet from the river water, dove into their food, as hungry as starving little wolves.

In the afternoon, the men formed teams and played baseball. The women put their small children down for naps and fanned away the heat and the flies from their sleeping children as they visited.

Mrs. Martin, that black-eyed Sass's mother, came by to visit with Aunt Olivia, bringing along her light-skinned daughter. She smiled, introducing her to Maggie Rose as Josephine. "But we call her Jo."

The girl smiled and sat down beside her. Maggie Rose could think of nothing to say to the girl who was nearly as white as she was, but a colored girl all the same. A long, uncomfortable silence grew between them, and Maggie Rose alternated between searching for something to say and chiding herself for thinking she had to say anything at all to a colored girl.

Finally, the silence grew too loud to bear and Maggie Rose had to say something, so she said, "I like your dress. It is very pretty." Actually, she thought, the bright-yellow dress with small white flowers embroidered down the front of the waist was much prettier than her own faded blue print.

"My sister, Annie, made it for me," the girl said. "She sews all the time. I kind of like to knit. But I like cooking best."

"Aunt Olivia is teaching me to cook," Maggie Rose said.

"My mother's teaching me," Jo said, smiling. "She's a wonderful cook."

Maybe it was the girl's bright, chirpy smile that made her say, "My mother is dead."

"Oh!" The air rushed out of the girl in that one word, and her eyes widened. "Oh, oh. I...I be so sorry," she stammered.

"Thank you," Maggie Rose answered. She shouldn't have said that. It was mean of her and, in a way, she was sorry. But she was a little miffed, too. *Was she supposed to like this girl because she looked so white? If not, then why didn't they trot out the darker girl? The sassy one?*

They sat again in silence, Jo creasing pleats in the full skirt of her pretty dress, her eyes fastened on the task she'd set for herself. When the silence had again grown to the unbearable stage, the girl looked up and a light came into her eyes. Turning quickly to her mother, she said, "Mama, Ruth Coker's over there." She inclined her head toward another black girl standing a few feet away and talking to someone sitting on a blanket. "Might I be excused to speak to her?" She turned back to Maggie Rose. "She's my friend," she offered.

Relieved to be rid of the girl, Maggie Rose said, "You ought to go see her then."

"Miss Goodwin might like to go 'long," Mrs. Martin said.

"Oh, no," Maggie Rose said quickly. "That's all right. I'll stay here."

Aunt Olivia gave her an odd searching look and said, "Would you watch the baby then? Mrs. Martin and I thought we'd go about visiting with some of the other ladies." She smiled down at Sally Ann who still slept, a chubby fist tucked under one round, smooth cheek.

As she sat beside the baby waving a hand at a persistent fly, Maggie Rose saw Hattie move among the blankets, stopping at some for a few minutes and moving on again. As Hattie stepped past the last blanket, a huge colored man came up to her. They talked awhile and then parted—the man walking now in Maggie Rose's direction.

Watching him, she thought he looked like a huge black bear, except for the frizzled mass of graying hair topping his head. As he passed close by, she saw with a shock that beneath the fierce, dark eyes, a large X had been branded in the skin of one cheek. She shivered. *How barbaric!* Why would a man mutilate himself? Was it some awful African ritual? Grandmother always said the Africans were at heart a heathen people who learned what civilized ways they had from the whites. Now, she could believe it.

Many of the women had makeshift tenting for a little shade over their blankets. Over theirs, Uncle Caleb had several gunny sacks sewn together, stretched over three stakes he'd pounded into the ground. Watching Sally Ann sleep in the shade of the sacks made Maggie Rose sleepy, too. She dozed off, waking with a jerk and an urgent need to pass water. Aunt Olivia had pointed out the small wooden outhouses when they first arrived. Set at the edge of the grounds near the wagons and screened off by a thick stand of what Aunt Olivia said were plum bushes, there was one for the men and boys to use and one for the women and girls.

She was beginning to feel uncomfortable and nearly ready to burst when Aunt Olivia returned. Feeling as if every eye was on her, Maggie Rose hurried toward the small wooden buildings, wishing she could suddenly sink out of sight.

The women's building was occupied, the latch fastened. She stood back to wait, and in a few seconds the door opened, and the black girl, Sass, and her Indian-looking friend stepped out. They were laughing, but the instant they saw her, their laughter faded.

Maggie Rose ducked her head and would have stepped past them, but the one called Sass said, "How do you like our Celebration?"

"F-fine," she stammered and tried again to go past them.

"We're going to the river to cool off. We can wait for you, if you want to go."

"I-I…" The invitation caught her completely by surprise. If she'd have had time to think, she thought later, she might have gone with them, if only for something to do. But flustered and confused, she hadn't been able to think of anything but getting back to the safety of the blanket. Gesturing vaguely back the way she had come," she stammered, "Ah…Aunt Olivia said to come right back."

Sass shrugged. "Suit yourself." She turned to her friend, "Come on, Mary." Scorn pulled her face into a sneer. "Guess Miss Uppity White Girl's wanting to be by herself."

The small, husky noise the Indian girl made, sounded like a laugh to Maggie Rose, and a blaze of red-hot anger roared inside her head. Turning away from the two girls, she jerked up the latch on the door and stepped inside.

~ Chapter Eight ~

SASS

I told you she'd not want to do anything with us," Sass said, as she and Mary walked toward the river and away from the Celebration grounds. "She thinks 'cause she's white, she's better than us." Gritting her teeth, Sass smacked a rounded fist into the palm of her other hand. "She do make me spittin' mad...that... that Miss Uppity White Girl," she sputtered.

"Oh, Sass," Mary said. "Why're you lettin' it bother you? She's just an o' white girl don't know no better."

"Mama said to try being friendly, but not to worry if she acted rude. Jo tried and the girl was awful to her." She did not add that her mother had also said that she thought being around colored folks was a little upsetting for the girl, and she probably just needed more time to adjust. Miss White Girl hadn't acted upset, just now, Sass thought. *She'd just acted uppity and rude.*

Mary grinned. "What you think your Mama gonna say if she catch you calling that girl 'Miss Uppity White Girl' like you just did?"

Sass grinned. "I 'spect she'll say, 'Girl, don't you be lettin' me hear words like that coming out o' your mouth, or you gonna be scrubbin' the kitchen floor 'til it clean enough to eat off of.'"

"Good thing she don't hear you then," Mary said, her dark eyes dancing.

Sass laughed, her anger at the white girl gone. Mary was right. Miss Maggie Rose Goodwin was nothing but an o' white girl and not worth getting all upset about.

At the river, Sass and Mary walked downstream from where the small children played in the shallow waters at the river's edge, under the watchful eyes of big brothers and sisters.

Farther on the river narrowed, and the waters were deeper. When they came to where a big, old, dead cotton-wood tree had fallen across the river, its roots pulled from the ground, Mary said, "Let's climb up on it," and began looking for a place to climb around the tangle of roots.

"I can see it fine from here," Sass said.

"Come on," Mary called, already past the roots and out on the trunk of the tree.

Sass watched her squat among the barren branches of the cottonwood, and with a little shiver of dread, climbed up after her. As she squatted beside Mary, she tried not to look at the river flowing deep and quiet beneath her. She had always been afraid of deep water. She didn't mind water to put her feet in, but she sure didn't like being over a whole big river. What if she slipped and fell in? *She'd drown that's what she'd do.*

She grew dizzy and closed her eyes, but still she could "see" the water flowing beneath her. She opened her eyes and grew dizzier still, as the tree seemed to suddenly start moving upstream, faster and faster. It didn't help that she was hanging on for dear life to the branches; they were brittle and weak and could easily break under her hand. She tried again to shut her eyes, but the tree still seemed to race upstream, and she felt as if she were losing her balance. She snapped her eyes open and, blinking rapidly, looked up at the blue sky. The dizziness eased, and the tree stopped moving. Blinking rapidly and keeping her eyes away from the water, kept the tree still, but the deep water, flowing so quietly below, drew her eyes like a beckoning hand. And as soon as she looked, the tree again seemed to move upstream.

"Be a good place to fish," Mary said. "Fish like hidin' back in under logs where it be deep and quiet."

Sass tried to nod, panic rising, her throat so dry she could not speak. *She had to get off. She couldn't stand it any longer!* She turned and, on hands and knees, scrambled back along the log and down over the tangle of roots, desperate for the safety of land.

"You be doing all right?" Mary asked from behind her.

"F...fine." She'd tried to keep her voice steady, but it had come out shaky.

"Oh," Mary said.

Mary knew. In that shaky voice she had given herself away.

"I'm ready to go, too," Mary said, coming up behind her. "Sure did think o' Mr. Fish would be down under there, but he don't 'pear to be."

Sass knew Mary was letting her save face, pretending not to notice the fear that still clung to her, but was fading now—the strength coming back to her weak, wobbly legs.

They walked past the dead cottonwood and farther upriver, keeping to the bank. The smooth flow of water made a gentle gurgling sound as it flowed past them, and she felt silly to have been so afraid, for it seemed perfectly harmless, now. Still, she walked on the side of Mary that kept her friend next to the water's edge. And after a while, her thoughts returned to the Goodwin girl and the certainty that she would not be going to their school. "I bet Miss Uppity White Girl won't be coming to school this fall," she said, squinting against the sun to look at Mary.

Mary shrugged. "So who be caring?"

"Not me," Sass said.

They had come to where the river had spread out wide and shallow, and Mary, suggesting they go wading, sat down on the ground to pull off her moccasins.

For a second, Sass saw the deep flow of water under the old, dead cottonwood and shivered. But she wasn't afraid where the water was shallow and, stepping out of her shoes, she joined Mary in the ankle-deep water. A small leaf floated down toward her, and she reached out and caught it.

Mary walked out into deeper water, pulling her skirts up with one hand. Now, in up to her knees, a grin lighting her face, she bent, and cupping water with a sideways motion of her hand, splashed a small spray on Sass.

Sass ignored the sprinkles of water. She was thinking about the Goodwin girl again. Even though she tried not to think about the uppity white girl, she couldn't keep her from coming to mind. "She sure do make me mad, " she said, kicking a spray of water ahead of her.

She hadn't realized she'd spoken aloud until Mary said, "You thinking 'bout that white girl again? Why you bother 'bout her? Do you think she be wastin' time worryin' about you?" Mary walked into deeper water, pulling her skirts higher up on her legs.

"Don't s'pose so," Sass answered. "We're probably all just a bunch of colored no-accounts who ought to still be slaves to people like her." Lifting her skirts higher, she waded out a few more cautious steps.

65

"Probably so," Mary said cheerfully, "but we don't be slaves no more." She took two or three more steps and, bending forward, hit the heel of her hand on the water's surface. The spray showered Sass.

"Hey! You got my dress all wet," Sass cried, a pretend scowl on her face.

"My. My. Ain't that just awful?" Mary mocked, her black eyes dancing with mischief. "You sound like Miss Uppity White Girl 'stead of my friend, Sass."

"And you," Sass retorted, "sound like some low-bred, no-account colored girl to me."

Mary laughed and waded closer to Sass. "Don't you mean some low-bred, no-account, redskin-colored girl?"

"Oh, and that too," Sass said cheerfully and, letting her skirt drop into the water, dipped in both hands and splashed Mary with a soaking spray.

Mary let go of her own skirts and they splashed each other and laughed until both were soaked to the skin.

They gave in together, running out of the water, their dresses hanging heavy and slapping wet against their legs. "That o' river sure cools a body off," Mary said, as she pulled up her skirts and began wringing out some of the river water. She grinned at Sass. "Bet it even cooled off your mad toward that white girl."

"I guess it did," Sass said. She watched Mary drop her skirts and wiggle her feet into her moccasins. In many ways, Sass thought, Mary was more Indian than colored. Her mother even tanned the hides she used to make their moccasins, low cut for summer and high-topped leggings with fringe for winter. Seth Melcher, an old bachelor, one of the original settlers of Solomon Town, brought the skins from the animals he trapped to Mary's mother, who made moccasins for him and for herself and Mary. The surplus skins, the old man took to Prairie City to sell.

The sun had nearly dried their dresses by the time they got back to the Celebration grounds. As they drew near, they spied Miss Julia Hardy standing back away from the crowd. Since the white people had come, she stayed along the fringes of the Celebration, leaning on her walking stick—watching, but never joining the festivities. The Bensens made sure she got a plate of food at mealtimes. When she finished eating, the old woman would leave her plate on the ground and move off to lean again on her walking stick, her black eyes ever watching. When it grew dark, she'd hurry home, her long cape flapping about her.

Last year, watching Miss Julia hurry home, Mary said, "She look like a bird going home to roost."

Sass had agreed. Now she looked across the Celebration grounds to where the old woman stood leaning on her cane, her black cape closed around her. The image of a big, black buzzard waiting, came to mind. She noticed the white girl and her aunt standing with Mrs. Mars, who was holding the Goodwin baby. She turned to look again at Miss Julia, and it seemed to her that the old woman was staring straight at the two white women and Miss Uppity. A little shiver of apprehension shot through her, raising gooseflesh on her skin.

~ *Chapter Nine* ~

MAGGIE ROSE

Uncle Caleb had carved a series of large, round, wooden beads and strung them on a string for Sally Ann to play with, and Maggie Rose amused the baby for a time by pulling the string of beads across the little girl's legs and up and around her neck and shoulders. Aunt Olivia had been waiting for her to watch Sally Ann again when she got back to the blanket. "Uncle Caleb wants me to look at a horse with him," she said, as Maggie Rose sat down beside the baby. "Do you mind? I won't be gone long."

No, she didn't mind. In fact she was glad to have something to do. This Celebration Day was beginning to get terribly long, and there was still the night and half a day tomorrow to get through.

As she amused Sally Ann with the string of beads, she tried not to think about meeting Sass Martin and her Indian friend at the outhouse. Her cheeks still burned at the memory of the colored girl's scornful words. "Miss Uppity White Girl" she'd called her. What nerve, speaking like that to her! No wonder she was called Sass. She had no business being so nasty, just because she hadn't wanted to go with them to the river. Miss Sassy Face couldn't have known that Aunt Olivia hadn't really asked her to come right back. It was true she should have gone, and if those girls had been white, she would have gone in a minute. But having colored girls offer their friendship had been just too unsettling and so confusing, she hadn't been able to think. This was such an odd place, this Solomon Town, where a colored girl was so bold as to say things like that to a white girl. *My goodness! In Georgia, she could get herself in a bushel of trouble carrying on like she was better than a white girl. Maybe these coloreds, here, all thought they were better than white folks. Maybe...* So engrossed in thinking about the two girls, she did not see Hattie and a man approach, until their shadows fell across the blanket, and she looked up into the woman's smiling face.

"Hello, Miss Maggie Rose," Hattie said. "You gettin' all settled in with your aunt and uncle?"

Startled, she barely squeaked out a, "Yes." She recognized the colored man beside Hattie as one of the men who had sung a solo this morning. Was he Hattie's beau? He must be, the way he was holding her arm, and the way she was looking up at him, smiles all over her face. "Yes," she said again in a steadier voice.

"The Martins sure are makin' me feel to home," Hattie volunteered.

Maggie Rose could not think of a thing to say to this woman she'd known all of her life, but had never really known. It was a shock to hear this once silent woman actually trying to carry on a conversation—and smiling too.

"That's nice," she finally said.

The smile disappeared from Hattie's face and her usual somber manner returned as she introduced the man with her. Maggie Rose missed the name. Parsnips...Parched...Preacher...

Something. Well, it didn't matter anyway.

The man bowed slightly. "I'm pleased to meet you, Miss," he said.

Maggie Rose nodded. She couldn't think of any words to say to this colored man.

Hattie, still unsmiling, drew herself up straighter, taller. "Goodbye, Miss Maggie Rose," she said and turned to look up at the man.

He nodded at Maggie Rose, and they walked away.

Staring after them, she was unaware that her aunt stood beside her until she spoke.

"Did Hattie introduce you to her friend?" Aunt Olivia asked.

"Yes." For some reason it made her feel odd to talk about Hattie and that man. *Would they get married? My goodness, they were both so old... forty at least.* To change the subject she asked, "Did Uncle Caleb buy the horse?"

Aunt Olivia chuckled. "Oh, no." She picked up Sally Ann and, draping the baby's small blanket over her shoulder and the front of her dress, she unbuttoned a few buttons to let the baby nurse. "I reminded him that the store and work at home keeps him so busy, he'd never have time to ride it, and it would just get fat and sassy on him." The smile on her face broadened. "He does have a weakness for horses, like I do for hats. If I were to look in Miss Reed's millinery shop, I'd think I just had to have a new hat, and yet I know the ones I have are quite serviceable."

Maggie Rose would never have thought that grown people would long for something they couldn't or shouldn't have. It was decidedly surprising.

When the supper hour arrived, Maggie Rose went to the river with Uncle Caleb to retrieve the big crock Aunt Olivia had filled with leftovers from the noon meal, and a gallon of lemonade she'd saved for their supper.

The perishable foods were kept cool in the river, set down in the water in crocks and jars and weighted down with stones on the lids. Maggie Rose saw Sass, her sister Jo, and the other older sister she had heard someone call Annie. All three girls were lifting crocks and jars from the river.

After supper, the evening's festivities began with a musical depicting the settling of Solomon Town. Aunt Olivia explained that the play and the original songs had been written the first year of the Celebration and not only told the story of the slaves' emancipation, but also commemorated the settling of Solomon Town. "Mr. Martin is always the narrator, as he has such a fine voice." She paused and looked over at Maggie Rose, a quizzical little expression on her face. "Did I tell you that Mr. Martin owns the newspaper here? The *Solomon Gazette*. Wasn't your daddy a newspaper man?"

Maggie Rose acknowledged that he was. She'd had no idea what Mr. Martin did for a living, but owning a newspaper would have been one of her last guesses. So she and Miss Sassy did have something in common after all, she thought with a rueful little grimace, which she hoped passed for a smile.

"And Mr. James Parsons, whom you met with Hattie," Aunt Olivia continued, "will sing several numbers. He's very talented, as you probably remember from hearing him this morning."

Maggie Rose nodded. So that was his name. She didn't want to talk about Hattie and her Mr. James Parsons. It embarrassed her to remember how she had acted when they had stopped by to talk to her. She had acted as if she hadn't a brain in her head. Like she was the colored person, humble and ignorant of good manners, while they stood over her, acting as if they were better than she was. At the very least, she should have stood up and looked them in the eye. After all, she was the white person.

At first Maggie Rose wasn't interested in the play. But the story of how the first settlers had come to Kansas, ex-slaves all, to settle this wild prairie land, soon captured her full attention.

In song and actions and narrations, the stories were told. The first narrator, accompanied by a trio of singers, told of how, without enough trees for lumber to build houses, they'd dug homes in the ground, living, the song said, like foxes in their dens. The next was a song, sung by Hattie's James Parsons. It told of the winter snows and the specter of starvation that haunted their dugouts. They had arrived in August, and the hot searing sun and the lateness of the season had prevented them from raising even a garden, let alone field crops. That winter, while wolves howled in the wind-driven snow, they'd prayed and pleaded to God to save them. "And," Hattie's beau sang, "He did." The man then sang how the Lord came, not in person, or in a mira-cle, (like the manna that literally fell from the skies when the Biblical people were lost in the wilderness), but as a band of Osage Indians who, seeing their dire situation, left meat enough for them to survive the winter.

George Martin was the next narrator. Two women with strong, deep voices sang a chorus each time he finished a segment of his talk. He told of a grasshopper invasion—the insects like huge black clouds, blocking out the sun. They had dropped from the sky to blanket the land—a crawl-ing, hopping mass that ate every growing thing, from field crops and vegetable gardens to blades of grass and leaves from trees. Then they moved on to the non-edibles: handles of pitchforks, shovels, and scythes, leather on harnesses and buggy seats, and if some woman had been unfortunate enough to have her family's clothes on the line, those, too, were soon eaten full of holes, leaving tatters of cloth flapping in the wind. And he told how, through it all, the people stayed, and by their grit and grim determination, Solomon Town came into being.

At the end of the program, George Martin announced a new closing song. "Mr. James Parson has written it for the next development that waits just around the bend for Solomon Town—a song of the railroad."

Everyone clapped and whistled and shouted when James Parsons finished his new song. It ended with some small boys up on the stage beside him—chanting, *chug, chug, chug,* as their little arms mimicked the rotation of wheels, fast and faster, and then slower and slower, and ending with a hissing as if of steam.

The sun had disappeared beneath the horizon by the time the musical was over. Aunt Olivia stood up and, handing Sally Ann to Maggie Rose, picked up the blanket and folded it. Around them the other women were doing the same. "The dancing is next," Aunt Olivia said, smiling. "Those of us without our wagons here lay our blankets in a pile and sort them out before we go home."

The benches, chairs, and stools were moved out to the edge of the dance area, and the men who, earlier, had played their musical instruments, and Clara Ruggles, the woman who had played Mrs. Mar's pump organ, began to play lively, toe-tapping tunes. Soon several couples were out on the hard-packed, dirt dance floor.

Aunt Olivia, with Sally Ann in her arms, sat down on one of the benches to watch the dancing, and Maggie Rose stood behind her. Uncle Caleb visited a while with some of the men and then came over to ask Aunt Olivia to dance.

Holding Sally Ann, Maggie Rose watched her aunt and uncle twirl about the dance floor. She thought they looked so handsome and graceful and felt a small surge of pride. When the dance was over, Aunt Olivia came back to hold the baby, and Uncle Caleb insisted that Maggie Rose take what he called "a spin around the floor."

Protesting that she had never danced before, Uncle Caleb told her there was no time like the present to learn. At first she stumbled a lot, feeling clumsy and awkward. Her cheeks burned with embarrassment, certain those dark-eyed people all watched only her. The crowd, lining the edges of the dance floor, clapped and swayed to the music, and when anyone laughed, Maggie Rose was sure they laughed at her. Finally, though, the music sort of took over, and her clumsy feet picked up the steps and the rhythm and she began to enjoy it. Once, as she twirled by on Uncle Caleb's arm, she saw the Martin girl, Sass, dancing with her Indian-looking friend. The Martins were dancing too, as was their daughter Jo on the arm of a serious-faced boy as dark as she was light. The boy's labored, clumsy steps were almost painful to watch. Maggie Rose felt a touch of sympathy, knowing that was probably how she had looked before she caught on to the steps. As Uncle Caleb swept her past the two, Maggie Rose turned her head so she'd not have to acknowledge the girl.

When Uncle Caleb escorted her back to the bench where Aunt Olivia sat, she saw Hattie and her beau standing in the middle of the dance floor, waiting for the music to begin again. It shocked her that they were holding hands. She looked away and caught a glimpse of the man she had seen earlier in the day, the man with the X on his cheek. She shivered. My, but he was a frightening-looking man. He scared her just to look at him, and yet she couldn't keep from looking. She thought it was kind of like having a wild wolf prowl outside your home. Even if you knew it couldn't get in, you'd still spend most of your time at the window, watching. Eventually, though, not seeing the wolf, you would go back to whatever had occupied you before. And it was when she forgot that he came up beside her.

Uncle Caleb and Aunt Olivia were out on the dance floor again, and holding Sally Ann, she'd stood up to watch Robbie and Bennie dance together, their little arms pumping, their feet half-skipping, half-jumping and way off beat to the music. Uncle Caleb and Aunt Olivia had just danced by, and Sally Ann waved her little arms at them. Suddenly, she felt a movement beside her and, turning her head, she looked up into the man's dark, burning eyes.

"Miss..." he began, but that was all she heard. Sally Ann clasped to her chest, she whirled and pushed through the crowd, silent screams echoing inside her head.

~ *Chapter Ten* ~

SASS

S ass, dancing with her brother, looked up in time to see the new teacher approach the white girl. She thought he said something and realized he had scared the girl, for she jerked back like she'd seen a ghost and, clutching the baby, disappeared into the crowd. "Oh, my," Sass muttered. "Oh, my."

A frown gathering, Jimmy growled, "What's the matter with you?"

"Nothing." She leaned out from Jimmy's arms to try to catch a glimpse of the girl, but she was gone, swallowed up in the crowd.

Jimmy's frown became a scowl. "What's squirming 'round in you?" he demanded. "I told Mama I'd dance with you, but not if you goin' to go actin' the silly fool."

"Oh, go find someone else to dance with," she retorted and not even waiting for Jimmy to escort her to the edge of the dance floor, she pulled away and hurried off in search of Mary. *This was just too good to keep.*

"You look like a coyote smack in the middle of a pen full of lambs," Mary said when Sass ran up to her and, grabbing her hand, pulled her back behind the crowd lining the dance floor.

"Oh, Mary, you should've seen her!" Sass chuckled gleefully. "Miss Uppity White Girl just got a look at Mr. Jacobs. Scared her near to death. Papa says she's going to our school. Just wait 'til she finds out Mr. Scary Black Man, with the brand on his face, is our new teacher."

"Well, of course she was scared," Mary said. "He'd scare anybody not knowin' him. I bet you'd be scared, too, if a big o' white man come up to you, lookin' all wild-eyed and scar-faced."

"Maybe." Sass kicked at a small clump of grass, all the joy pushed out by darker thoughts. *That girl—that white girl—so high up on her 'better-than-you-are' horse, who couldn't even walk down to the river with them today, didn't deserve any sympathy, and here Mary was siding with Miss Uppity against her... her very own best friend.*

She brought her head up and scowled at Mary. "Well, she ought to know she'd be safe with people all around her. She's just a big fraidy-cat."

Mary shrugged. "My mother thinks she most likely be shy and little bit nervous. She says it'd be like us if we got sent to live in a white town. Makes me wonder about when those Osage Indians come 'long and saved your people that first winter. Bet those little colored children lookin' out of their dugouts be some scared seein' a big Indian standing there in the snow."

"*Your* people?" Sass said. Her ears had fastened on those two words so the rest of what Mary said, barely registered. *Was Mary denying her own colored blood in siding with that white girl?* "What do you mean? They're *your* people too. Are you going to turn into an Indian now and not be colored at all?" She heard the cold edge of anger in her voice and felt the sting of quick, hot tears behind her eyes.

"Oh, Sass!" Mary's face softened, and she reached out and touched Sass's arm. "I'm awful sorry. I didn't mean ..."

"I know." Sass ducked her head, ashamed of herself. She was always so quick to find fault in others. Mary looked on both sides of a person, the good and the bad, and tried to see more of the good side. She looked again at Mary and a sudden thought brought a grin spilling across her face. "Think we ought to tell Miss White Girl 'bout the new teacher before school starts? I can see her stepping into the school house and seeing him, jump and run like a scared rabbit all the way back home."

Mary chuckled. "Let's leave her aunt and uncle tell her. Don't believe we need to be doing it." She was silent for a while, and then said, "I didn't mean those first settlers just be your people. I guess 'cause my daddy's gone and Mama's Indian, I start to think of myself as mostly Indian."

"I guess I would, too," Sass said, a new thought popping into her head. "Is your mother Osage? If she is, then her people rescued your father's people that first winter."

Mary smiled. "My mother's people be Cheyenne, a whole different tribe, so I guess it don't count."

"'Course it counts," Sass said. "Indian is Indian, just as colored is colored. In Africa they have tribes, just like Indians do, but we're still all from the Negro race. Whites have tribes, too, though they don't call them that."

"Really?" Mary's brows arched in disbelief.

"Sure." Sass grinned. "The white tribes are called German and English and Italian and so on. Papa says there's a German settlement some forty to sixty miles from here, and right next to them, not more than ten to fifteen miles, is a town of Dutch people. He says they have their own language and their own churches, and they don't hardly mix with each other at all. And every one of them have white faces." Sass searched her memory for the names of other white people tribes and came up with Swedes, French, and Irish.

"A lot of others came to this country from other places across the ocean, or at least their ancestors did." She smiled, "Even Chinese, but they're not white, or colored either."

Mary smiled. "My Indian people might've come from somewhere else, too, but so long ago don't no one remember."

"Maybe," Sass said.

A gleam of mischief in her eyes and a haughty tilt to her chin, Mary said, "I think I'm from the two best races of all."

"So you're better than all of us," Sass teased, a mock frown on her face. "Guess I'll just call you Miss Perfect, then, all right?"

"Sure," Mary returned her grin. "And I'll call you Miss Not-Quite-as-Good-as-Me. How 'bout that?"

"It'll be all right with me, girl," Sass said, "if you want me yanking those long braids out of your head and scratching out your eyes."

Mary laughed. "Noooooooo, thank you." She turned to watch the people dancing, one foot beginning to tap to the music. "Let's go dance some more 'fore they get to intermission time.

"It's startin' to get dark. Makes the lanterns on the stage look awful pretty, don't you think? "

"Sure brings in the bugs, though," Sass said.

Sass danced with Mary and then Joseph Cantwell. Jimmy, with prodding from Mama, Sass was sure, asked Mary.

After that dance, the musicians laid down their instruments, and everyone crossed the grounds to where the women had set out jugs of cool lemonade and the leftovers from dinner. They had carried the benches over, but most sat on the ground, or stood, talking as they ate—their voices in competition with the near constant drone of the locust among the trees and grasses. It was full dark now, and thousands of fireflies fitted about, their flickering lights like minute-size lanterns constantly being turned on and off.

The smaller children, tired and sleepy, had gone to their mother's arms, or in sleep had slipped down to lie huddled at a parent's feet. Sass saw Robbie Goodwin and Joseph's little brother, Amos, chasing after the fireflies. Bennie Goodwin, looking sleepy-eyed, was sucking the two middle finger of his right hand, as he leaned against his mother's skirts. Olivia Goodwin sat on one of the school benches between two colored mothers, and Sass thought that now, in the darkness with only the lights from the lanterns, they looked much the same. Olivia Goodwin's blond hair and pale skin, darkened in the night's shadows, no longer looked so much different from the dark-faces beside her.

Smiling at her thoughts, Sass looked about for the rest of the Goodwin family. Caleb Goodwin stood near the stage visiting with Mr. Parsons and her own daddy.

Maggie Rose stood alone. For the space of a heartbeat, Sass felt a touch of sympathy for the girl. She started to turn to Mary to ask if she thought they should try again to be friendly to her, when the music started up again and she decided the girl would most likely be going back to hold the Goodwin baby anyway, so that her aunt and uncle could dance.

A three-quarter moon was far into the sky when the dance was over. Sass and Mary walked past the Goodwin wagon as they started for home. Caleb Goodwin had walked home to get their wagon and was now putting his youngest son, who was sound asleep, on a blanket in the back beside Maggie Rose. They passed by close enough for the white girl to recognize them, but if she did, she gave no sign.

~ *Chapter Eleven* ~

MAGGIE ROSE

As she rode home from the Celebration in the back seat of Uncle Caleb's mule-drawn wagon, Maggie Rose wished that either she or that Sass girl would take sick in the night, so one of them would not be at the Celebration tomorrow. It wouldn't have to be anything more than a cold, and she would gladly suffer a runny nose and sneezes and coughs not to see that sassy girl again. But the next morning, she felt as well as ever and, as soon as they arrived at the Celebration grounds, the Martins came up to greet them. Of course, Miss Sassy Face was with them, looking perfectly healthy.

Mr. and Mrs. Martin visited with Uncle Caleb and Aunt Olivia a few minutes and then, right out of the blue, Mr. Martin turned to his sassy-faced daughter. "Why don't you and Miss Goodwin sit together for the church service?"

Miss Sassy's head jerked up in surprise, and the look on her face left no doubt about how she felt about that suggestion. It amused Maggie Rose and made her mad at the same time. Mrs. Martin had tried to stick her with that white-looking daughter of hers, and now Mr. Martin was trying to get her with this sassy one. She wondered why the Indian girl hadn't shown up this morning. Last night, she had asked Aunt Olivia about Mary. "She has an Indian mother," Aunt Olivia told her, "but her father was colored. She certainly favors her mother though."

"She sure does," Maggie Rose said. "In fact, she doesn't look colored at all."

"It's like Jo, the Martin's middle daughter," Aunt Olivia said. "Mr. Martin had several white ancestors, which accounts for his lighter eyes and complexion. That white strain appears to have come out in his middle daughter."

Now, Maggie Rose eyed the Martin family, all colored looking except the one called Jo. Even Mr. Martin, although he had gray eyes and his skin was quite light, still looked colored. She couldn't imagine why a white person would want to marry a colored one, but evidently some did.

Aunt Olivia reclaimed her attention with a cheery, "See you after the service," and walked away with Uncle Caleb and the Martins, leaving her with Miss Sassy Face.

"Well, let's find a seat," Miss Sassy Face said, a frown wrinkling her brow and narrowing her dark eyes.

They walked, without speaking, to the seating set up in rows for the church service and found a place on the end of one of the school benches on the back row. Around them, people laughed and talked as they moved in and took up seats.

Maggie Rose watched Sass out of the corner of her eye. The girl sat straight and stiff, staring straight ahead.

A fly began to buzz about Maggie Rose. She swatted at the fly, but it would not leave her alone. At the same time, Miss Sassy Face started jiggling her legs up and down under her long brown skirt. Up and down and up and down. The fly disappeared, but this new irritation was worse. *If she doesn't stop it soon, I'm going to smack her.* She almost laughed at the thought, for she knew Miss Sassy Face wouldn't run off to her mama. Oh, no. She'd smack her right back, and there they'd be—smacking each other and pulling hair and maybe even rolling on the ground. The Reverend would get up and try to start his sermon, but the people wouldn't be listening. They'd all be craning their necks to see what was making all the commotion. That image started the giggles in Maggie Rose. To keep them at bay, she turned to Sass and tried to speak seriously, but a little snicker squeezed around her words. "Where's that girl you're usually with?"

The colored girl frowned.

She thinks I'm laughing at her. Again Maggie Rose tried to control the giggles, but she could not shut out the image of them rolling around on the ground, and another giggle squeezed out with her next words, "That Mary girl."

Sass's frown deepened, and she said in a frost-coated voice, "Her mother was needing help. One of the old people she takes care of took sick in the night."

"Oh," Maggie Rose said, the giggles subsiding. *So someone did get sick after all—just the wrong someone.*

Silence again fell between them. So what to say now? She thought of the girl's odd name and asked, "Is Sass your real name?"

"No, it's Evangeline," Sass's voice was still chilled.

Maggie Rose felt a little jolt of surprise. *Had she been named for Henry Wadsworth Longfellow's 'Evangeline'? The girl in his poem about the Acadian people driven from their home and forced to settle in a new land?* Grandmother always said coloreds were too stupid to learn to read. But Sass's father put out the weekly newspaper, so maybe Grandmother was wrong about that. "That's a pretty name," she said. "If it were mine, I'd want to be called that instead of Sass."

"Well, I like to be called Sass," the girl said.

Not only frosty, but prickly as a thorny, old rose bush, too. "I just meant it's a little unusual," she said.

"I suppose it is," Sass said, her voice still like thorns, iced with glittering frost.

Maggie Rose looked around at the gathering congregation and wondered how much longer before the service started. She wished that preacher or whoever got this thing going would hurry. She looked down at her fingers, absently twisting the ring Aunt Olivia had given her to wear, and wished the day to be over.

Beside her, Sass made a little throat-clearing sound and said, "The day I was born, my father came in to look at me in Mama's arms, and they say that just as he looked at me, I scrunched up my face and stuck out my bottom lip. It tickled him and he said. 'Well, hello, Miss Sassy.' The name just stuck—only it got shortened to Sass."

"Oh," Maggie Rose said. *If her father had said that to her, she would have wanted to be called that, too, but she wasn't going to say so to Miss Sassy.* The girl had thawed a little and the thorns were gone, but one wrong word and she'd probably get mad all over again.

Maggie Rose was relieved when, at last, a man dressed in black stepped up to the speaker's stand and called out, "Come, brothers. Come, sisters. Let us worship the Lord this beautiful morning." Behind him, Clara Ruggles began playing the pump organ, and a group of men and women started filing up on the stage, singing and clapping and swaying to the music. One of the men Maggie Rose recognized as Hattie's Mr. Parsons, and the song they were singing was something about swinging low on a chariot, whatever that meant.

The first part of the service with the music captivated Maggie Rose and, glancing sideways at Sass, she saw that she, too, was enjoying the songs. Then the black-coated preacher began the sermon. For a while Maggie Rose was entertained by the people who clapped and called out, *"Amen"* and other words like they were encouraging the minister. Often, they threw up their hands or stood to call out a word of praise to the Lord. But after a while, the bench grew hard, and even the loudest shouts no longer could keep her from yawning. She bet Miss Sassy Face was bored, too.

They ate the noon meal with all the Martins. Aunt Olivia motioned Maggie Rose to a seat by Sass. During the meal, the Martins and Uncle Caleb and Aunt Olivia talked so much no one seemed to notice that neither she nor Sass spoke a word to each other.

This meal ended the Celebration for another year, and Maggie Rose could hardly wait for Uncle Caleb to take them home. But it would be a while yet, Aunt Olivia told her, as the men all helped to clean up the grounds, get the pump organ loaded in Mr and Mrs. Mar's wagon, and take the benches back to the schoolhouse.

While they waited, Mrs. Martin and her two older daughters found a shady place to sit under a cottonwood, and Aunt Olivia joined them to nurse Sally Ann. The boy, Joseph, had again taken Robbie and Bennie along with his own little brothers to play by the river, until their families were ready to go home. Sass had left some time ago to go to her friend's house, not even bothering to say goodbye.

To pass the time, Maggie Rose decided to walk down to the river to watch the little boys play in the water. She was tired and anxious to go home. She smiled at the thought. She had called the sod house home. She had to admit she was as comfortable and happy there as if it *were* truly her home.

She thought about next fall when she would go to school in Prairie City, and Uncle Caleb would pay some strangers for her to live in their home. She hoped they would be nice, but at least they wouldn't be colored. She knew she would miss Uncle Caleb and Aunt Olivia and the children. But they would come to town sometimes, and maybe there would be times when she could go home for a while—maybe for Christmas.

Out of sight of the Celebration grounds, her thoughts on her new home, she was unaware of the black figure moving toward her. She screamed as it flew at her, its maw of a mouth uttering a rage of words that flooded her whole being with terror. She cowered before the huge, black bird-like creature, wings flapping as it hissed and screamed. She dropped to the ground, hunched over, her hands flying up to cover her face, as her own awful screams ripped from her throat.

Someone shouted, and enough of her senses came back to try to get away. She scrambled on all fours, her skirts tangling about her legs. Darting a look back over her shoulder, she saw that the creature wasn't a huge bird at all, but an old woman in a loose-flowing, ragged dress and a long black cape. She jumped to her feet and faced the woman, anger dissolving her fear. "You old witch!" she yelled. "What do you think you're doing?" She stood her ground as the woman moved toward her, a stout stick raised menacingly above a head wrapped in an old green and black rag, gray hair sprouting out from under it.

"You not wanted, white girl," the old woman hissed, her eyes black, burning orbs of hatred. "Git you white skin out o' here." She thrust her face close to Maggie Rose's and spit. The nasty wetness sprayed across her face, and she thought she'd throw up. Then blind rage swept over her, and she screamed out a torrent of words, "You old black hag! You nasty old thing! You...you...you old crone!"

She saw the walking stick raised high and as it came down, she ducked, and her hands came up to protect her head. The blow landed on her arms, but with little force, and a man yelled, "Miss Julia!"

Maggie Rose looked up. Mr. Martin had ahold of the old woman's arm and, bent close, was speaking to her in a firm, even voice. "She's a niece of the Goodwins," he said, "and has every right to be here."

Those left at the Celebration grounds now crowded around. Maggie Rose saw Uncle Caleb start toward them, and Aunt Olivia put out a hand to stop him.

"She bring troubles!" the woman snarled, her black eyes glaring her hatred past Mr. Martin to Maggie Rose.

"Nonsense," Mr. Martin said. "She's just a girl." The tone of his voice hardened. "If you harm her, or her family, you will be locked away in a white man's jail. Do you understand me?"

For an answer, the old woman jerked her arm from his grasp and stomped off, her walking stick jabbing the ground with each step, her black cape closed about her like bat wings.

Mr. Martin stared after the old woman a moment before turning back to Maggie Rose. "I'm sorry, Miss Goodwin. I don't know what set her off."

In a daze of fear, anger, and disgust, Maggie Rose could only nod. Then, among the gathered crowd, she saw Sass's round, dark face and big eyes. *She'd come back.* The Indian girl wasn't with her. She must still be needed at home. *Had she heard her screams? Had she seen her scrambling on all fours like some giant spider?* She was probably just about to laugh her head off and already thinking how she'd tell this story to her Indian friend. How they'd howl about her tangling with the old witch. Probably laugh until their sides ached. *Oh, those two made her mad enough to scream!*

"Maggie Rose?" Aunt Olivia touched her arm. "Would you run on down to the river and tell the boys their father's here, and we have to go now?"

Maggie Rose was grateful to her aunt for giving her something to do, so she would no longer be this dreadful center of attention. As she walked toward the river, images of the old, black crone went with her. Even though she knew it was silly—the woman was old and could do her no real harm—Maggie Rose could not help feeling a slight twinge of fear.

~ *Chapter Twelve* ~

SASS

The hot days of August slipped into September. The wild sunflowers grew tall, their heads heavy with bright blossoms, and the mottled pink and purple fruit of the wild plum waited, ready to be harvested for sweet jams and jellies.

Sass was excited about school. Mr. Jacobs would be an interesting teacher, far different from the gentle Miss Alexander who got married as soon as school was out last spring. Everyone said Mr. Jacobs had two big boxes of books to add to the school's meager collection. She hoped so, for she had read every book there, and some twice and three times. Everyone was also saying that Mr. Jacobs wouldn't be allowing any horse-play from the boys during school-time, and would be just the example needed to show their children how privileged they were to be allowed to learn.

She thought of that day in early spring when the man had arrived with his mule-drawn wagon to announce that if they needed a teacher, he was willing and able. Papa had liked him right off, and in visiting with him for the paper, had learned his story.

Born and raised a slave, he had been brought up from the slave cabins to the master's house to be a companion to their son, crippled since birth. Hoping the boy could attend a university some day, the parents had hired the best tutors for him. Mr. Jacobs, although not formally taught, was always in the room and learned along with the boy. After the lessons were over, the boy often lent him his slate, so he could practice his letters and sums.

"How did that brand get on his face?" Sass asked. "Did he have a bad master?" She and the other school-age children had all been wondering, and all having heard "slave" stories, had decided that was probably the case.

Papa nodded. "He told me the boy died at seventeen, never making it to college at all. After the boy's death, Mr. Jacobs was given a cot in the cellar and the job of tending the flower gardens and the grounds around the place. Every evening when he came in from his work, he passed by the master's library on the way to his cot in the cellar. The cellar was such a solitary place and, being used to the company of the boy, he was lonesome. He also missed having books to read, and he said he grew so hungry for something to read, that one day he dared to sneak a book out of the library to read by candlelight in his cellar room. Once again, he knew the pleasures of reading, but it was not to last. He handled the books carefully and returned them none the worse for his having read them, and he got by for several years before he was caught."

"What happened?" Sass spoke up, anxious to hear the rest of the story. "Is that how he got the brand on his face?"

"Yes. He said he never knew exactly what happened, but one day his master confronted him, shaking a book in his face. He was sent to the overseer, who took him down to the slave quarters and, strapping him down on the ground, branded that X on his cheek. From then on he was assigned to the stables."

Sass winced at the thought of the pain of that branding, and the humiliation of being treated like an animal, and felt the tears gather behind her eyes.

"I know," Papa said, giving her hand a squeeze of sympathy. "But he never gave up hoping that someday he would have access to books again, and when he was freed on Emancipation Day, he roamed the country doing odd jobs and collecting books."

"Did he have his wagon and mule then?" Sass asked.

"Not right away, but eventually he acquired them. And when he heard of Solomon Town—a town settled by ex-slaves—he said he knew he must come here and teach the children. That this was where he belonged."

In mid-September, Mr. Jacobs began visiting the homes of all of his students. Sass was certain that the white girl's aunt and uncle had told her that Mr. Jacobs was to be the new teacher. Still she wondered about his visit to the Goodwins.

As it turned out, on an errand for her mother to Mr. Goodwin's mercantile, Sass heard about it from Mrs. Goodwin and Mrs. Mars, who were at the store waiting while Mr. Goodwin finished with a customer. Realizing they were discussing Mr. Jacobs' visit to the Goodwin house, Sass pretended to look at several pairs of new shoes, black and shiny as polished coal, so she could stand near enough to hear what the women said.

"He was so formal, so very stiff and proper," Olivia Goodwin said. Sass heard a smile in her voice. "Maggie Rose was a little apprehensive about him. You know how he looks, especially with that brand on his cheek."

"You told her who he was before he came calling, didn't you?" Mrs. Mars asked.

"Oh, my, yes. He about scared her to death the Saturday night of the Celebration. When Caleb and I left the dance floor and came back to her and the baby, she was clutching Sally Ann and trembling with fright. We explained then who he was, and I mentioned the incident to him when he came the other day. He apologized. He told Maggie Rose he had no business approaching her, but it had just not occurred to him that she wouldn't know who he was. He had talked to a lot of the other children, encouraging them to come to school, as he was going to be their new teacher, and that the more children who attended, the happier that made him." She laughed. "He made it sound like they would be doing him a favor by coming to school."

"What did your little ones think of him?" Mrs. Mars asked.

"Oh, they were quite taken with him. Robbie was six last month so he'll be going to school, and poor Bennie's so jealous."

"And your niece?"

"I couldn't really tell. She doesn't want to go to school and tried to talk her uncle out of sending her. I could certainly use her help, but Caleb thinks it will help her adjust to life here."

"I imagine it will take some getting used to," Mrs. Mars said, nodding her head.

"Yes. Caleb says if she goes this year, he will send her to Prairie City next fall to the new normal school there. It's a secondary school to prepare students for teaching or to go on to a university. We hope to find a nice home where she can board while she's in school."

Mrs. Goodwin's words surprised Sass. *A normal school? To learn more?* For a moment it excited her, and then she came down from the clouds and back to solid earth.

Why did she even for half a second think <u>she</u> could go? If by some miracle, they would let her, a colored girl, into that school, she wouldn't be able to stay the night. She could just see herself, books in her arms, walking out of Prairie City toward the setting sun, to sleep in the dugout. So caught up in that image of her walking the road to the dugout, she jumped when the clock Mr. Goodwin kept on a shelf behind the counter struck two loud tones.

"My goodness," Mrs. Mars said. "I'd better get on over to the bank. I told Mr. Mars I'd be there by two, so I've got to run now. Goodbye, Caleb," she called, and with a quick wave of her hand, went out the door.

Olivia Goodwin turned back toward her husband and, in doing so, spotted Sass. "Well, my dear, Sass," she said, smiling. "I didn't see you come in. How is your mother and the rest of your family?"

"Just fine, Mrs. Goodwin." Sass returned her smile. She sure liked that white girl's aunt. Too bad Miss Uppity wasn't more like her.

"Has Mr. Jacobs called at your home, yet?" Olivia Goodwin asked.

"Yes, ma'am," Sass said, "several days ago."

"I expect you are anxious to get started to school again. Mary's going, too, isn't she?"

"Yes, ma'am," Sass answered. "She's planning to any-way—if her Mama's not going to need her help at home."

~ *Chapter Thirteen* ~

MAGGIE ROSE

Maggie Rose had never before known the work involved in getting food ready for the winter months. It seemed to her that she had sliced enough cabbages and cucumbers for the pickling crocks to feed Grandmother's whole, hated Yankee army. And soon, she'd have to help cut up the pig and the yearling calf that Uncle Caleb would butcher when it got colder this fall. They would also be making soap. One made soap, Aunt Olivia told her, from the fat saved at butchering time, wood ashes, and water— all boiled in a big kettle outside over a hot fire.

She dreaded the day when the gentle yearling, who loved to be scratched behind his ears, would be killed for his meat, and she was sure she'd never be able to eat a bite of him. But when she voiced her concern to Uncle Caleb, he just laughed.

"Don't worry," he said. "When the snow blows and it's freezing cold, you'll smell those savory juices cooking and by the time he gets to your plate, you'll see him only as supper."

Because of the work necessary to get crops harvested, food stored away for the winter, and the wild plums gathered for jams and jellies, school would not begin until the second week of October.

The first day, Maggie Rose was so nervous she could hardly keep her breakfast down. Aunt Olivia's ring had so far kept her from biting her nails, and the desire to do so was nearly gone. Her fingernails had grown out, and her fingertips were no longer sore, but this morning, scared and anxious, she'd chewed off the nail from one little finger before she'd realized it.

On the walk to school, she was grateful for Robbie's hand in hers. He was as excited and as happy about school as she was dreading it, and when they reached the school yard, he pulled his hand free and ran over to join a group of little colored boys.

Swallowing hard against the fear welling up inside her, Maggie Rose forced herself to walk towards the long, low sod schoolhouse. She'd glimpsed the Martin girl and her Indian friend behind her on the road, and she wanted to be inside and seated before they arrived. But she dreaded going inside almost as much as letting those two girls catch up with her.

Mr. Jacobs was at his desk, when she entered the building. "Good morning, Miss Goodwin," he said. "Please take a seat on one of the benches in the two back rows. The younger children need to sit towards the front." She seated herself at the far end of the last bench against the back wall of the soddy and wondered if anyone would sit next to her.

She felt as if every pair of dark eyes in the school looked at her, as they entered and took their seats. No one sat by her until a girl, who just escaped being tardy by seconds, stumbled past her classmates and flopped down with a sigh on the bench beside her. The girl's name, she learned later, was Nellie Spooner.

Mr. Jacobs called out the roll, making a mark in a narrow black book. Then, with a gesture toward a small

American flag on his desk, said, "I have this to remind you that you are all citizens of this country. You are all Americans, although some will treat you as less than human, let alone a citizen of this country. Some say we, who came as slaves, or are the descendants of slaves, ought to go back to Africa, but most of us were born here. Africa is more foreign to us than America. I don't want to go to Africa any more than those whose ancestors came from France or England or Germany want to go back to their respective countries. This is our homeland now, just as it is theirs. We all are Americans, none more so than the other, except the Indian, who is a native of this soil."

One of the two boys at the back of the room suddenly poked his friend and whispered something. Like a flash fire, Mr. Jacobs' eyes were on the boys. "Mr. Willy Shaw and Mr. Henry Davidson," Mr. Jacobs said in a voice soft as a feather-filled pillow, but strong as steel. "Do you have something you wish to add?"

"No, sir, Mr. Jacobs, " they replied in unison. And as if they thought the teacher deaf, repeated the words again in a louder voice, "No, sir, Mr. Jacobs."

"Before we start our lessons," Mr. Jacobs said, his eyes moving from the boys to take in the whole room, "lessons I can assure you we will be taking seriously from the youngest pupil to the oldest, I want to tell you a story." He moved out from behind his desk and sat on the edge of it, losing his formal manner, and the room, Maggie Rose thought, changed to a softer, friendlier place.

"In the deep South on a plantation, a small, colored boy grew up, and early on he loved the sounds of words..."

It was a little while before Maggie Rose realized he was talking about himself, and the story he told was sad and, at the end, horrifying.

Aunt Olivia and Uncle Caleb asked about school that evening at the supper table. Robbie talked about the fun he'd had at recess, and she told them about the book Mr. Jacobs had started reading aloud to them, the story of a horse called Black Beauty.

She couldn't yet speak of the brand on Mr. Jacobs' cheek. It had not been some African tribal ritual after all, but white people like herself who had done that awful thing, and just for reading a book. She'd thought of all of Miss Green's books she had sneaked past Grandmother and, while he was telling his story, had felt such a kinship to Mr. Jacobs that tears had nearly slipped over the edge of her eyes. The rest of the morning she had not been able to look at him, afraid somehow that he might think that she'd had a part in it—which was foolish, of course. She had not even been born when Mr. Jacobs was branded.

~ *Chapter Fourteen* ~

SASS

The first snow of the season was just a dry powder blown across the frozen ground in swirls of white. At the supper table, Mama told about seeing Mrs. Goodwin at the mercantile. Olivia Goodwin had told Mama that Miss Uppity White Girl (only she didn't call her that) had never seen snow before today.

"She's gettin' all excited now to see a big snow," Mama said, smiling at Sass and the others around the table. "The girl don't know it now, but she gonna be awful sick of snow and cold 'fore winter gets on by."

Sass thought about the white girl when the next storm passed through, leaving an inch or so of snow. She wondered if the girl would go out and play in it with the little boys. Probably, though, like Jo, she was too "lady-like" for that. *Too bad if she was, because she'd sure miss out on a lot of fun.*

On the way home from school that day she said as much to Mary.

"Everybody don't like to be playin' in the cold and snow," Mary said. "Don't mean she's not a nice person. Can't nobody tell, though, if she don't speak to nobody. Don't believe she even speakin' to Nellie sittin' right beside her."

"She won't even walk by me," Sass said, remembering with a hot swell of anger the times the girl had gone out of her way to avoid being near her. Once, she even waited to return a book to Mr. Jacobs' desk until Sass had returned the one she'd borrowed and was seated again.

"She's acting like she's too good to be speaking to coloreds," Sass complained that day to Mary.

"Don't be worryin' me none," Mary said with a small shrug. "How come it be so worrisome to you?"

"It's not," Sass declared. "I just don't like the way she acts. Like she's better'n us."

"Well, she don't be," Mary said, and, with a sudden grin, challenged her to a race to the end of the road.

When Sass got home from school, she sat behind the kitchen range warming herself and playing with Miss Muff's kittens.

"You'd best be findin' homes for those babies," Mama reminded her as she emptied a dish filled with small chunks of potatoes into the pot of vegetable soup she was cooking for their supper. "I won't be havin' this house filled up with cats."

Sass had been surprised when Mama allowed the cat to have her kittens in the house. "This weather, they gonna freeze fast as they born," Mama had said. Now every day Mama reminded her that she needed to find homes for the kittens.

"Mary's goin' take one," Sass said. "And I'll ask at school. But I've got a little time, don't I, Mama? They're just four weeks, now."

"Time's coming sooner'n you be thinkin', honey-girl." She stirred the pot of soup and laid the spoon down, lifting the end of her apron to wipe her hands. "You warmed all up now? I'm still needin' those crackers from Mr. Goodwin's store. He'll be closin' soon and, if you goin' to meet Papa and come home with him, you'd best get to scootin'."

Sass pulled on her mittens and shrugging into her coat, stepped out into the gathering darkness, then hurried up their road to the main street of Solomon Town. As she neared Mr. Goodwin's store, she saw someone coming from the opposite direction and knew by the gray coat and bright red muffler that it was Maggie Rose. *"Oh, happiness and joy!"* Sass muttered. "Miss Uppity White girl and me are going to meet right at the door."

She thought of turning back, but she knew her mother would have no patience with her coming home empty-handed. She broke into a run, the icy air whipping past her face. As she entered the warmth of the store, she glanced back. The Goodwin girl would be there in a few minutes; she'd no time to spare.

"Well, good evening, Miss Martin," Caleb Goodwin said as she rushed through the door. "What's your hurry? I don't close for a good half hour yet."

"Mama sent me for some soda crackers," Sass said, ignoring his question. She couldn't very well say, *I'm hurrying to get out of here 'cause your niece is coming.*

Caleb Goodwin seemed bound to move turtle slow getting the soda crackers and had to ask her all about school and tell her what his niece had said about it. Before he even had the crackers bagged, Miss Uppity was coming in the door. So, of course, he had to stop and greet her.

The girl acknowledged his greeting with one of her own as she unwound her muffler and slipped out of her coat. "Aunt Olivia sent me to walk home with you. She thought I needed the air." She spread her hands out to catch the warmth coming from the pot-bellied stove in the middle of the room, her tumble of long brown hair gleaming in the lamps Mr. Goodwin had lit against the gathering dusk.

Not once had she looked at Sass.

"She's trying to thicken up that Southern blood, so you'll make it through the winter," her Uncle Caleb said with a smile. Then his smile disappeared, and he gave her a funny look and turned to Sass. "What's going on here? Can't believe neither one of you are going to say hello?"

"Hello, Evangeline," Maggie Rose said.

"Hello, Miss Goodwin," Sass answered.

Caleb Goodwin snorted like a horse. "Evangeline? Miss Goodwin?" He lifted his brows in a mock look of surprise. "Evangeline? My goodness, don't tell me your parents have started calling you Evangeline?"

A small grin tugged at Sass's lips. "No, sir."

"Then why are you calling her that?" Mr. Goodwin said, turning to frown at Miss Uppity, who shrugged and mumbled that she didn't know.

"Your niece thinks Sass is a funny name," Sass volunteered.

Sass hid a small grin when the girl said, a hint of anger in her voice, "Well, I can't see why anyone in their right mind would want to be called Sass when Evangeline is such a pretty name."

"Oh, I see," Caleb Goodwin said, nodding his head several times. "I see. We have a spat of some kind going on here. Well, I expect you two will work it out." He looked at Sass, then at Maggie Rose, and shook his head again. Then he finished filling the sack with crackers and handed it to Sass. "Goodnight, Miss. I'll just add this to your Daddy's bill. Tell your dear family I send my greetings."

"I will, sir," Sass said. She felt bad about having him see her and his niece being hateful to each other. He was a friend of Papa's and a very nice man. "I'm going to meet Papa at the Gazette and walk home with him," she said, hoping he'd see that her not being able to get along with his niece had nothing to do with him. She darted a quick look at Miss Uppity, but the girl was staring at the stove and completely ignoring her. Mr. Caleb looked at his niece, as he came around from behind the counter and opened the door for Sass.

"Aren't you going to tell your schoolmate goodnight?" he asked.

"Good night," Miss Uppity said.

Sass responded with her own, "Good night," and went out the door. She fumed all the way over to Papa's office, and even his pleasure in seeing her could not erase the anger she carried with her. She could hardly wait for her father to blow out the lamps and lock up, so as they walked home, she could tell him about that rude, uppity white girl. But as they stepped outside and turned in the near dark toward home, the words she meant to say seemed to be stuck in her throat.

~ *Chapter Fifteen* ~

MAGGIE ROSE

After the colored girl left, Maggie Rose braced herself for a "talking to" from her uncle. But he went about closing up the store, speaking only to remind her to cover the counters with the long white covers he used to keep the merchandise clean and dust-free. He still hadn't said anything when they stepped out into the star-studded night to walk the snowy road home. But as they came in sight of the house, he said, "You and Miss Martin don't seem to be getting along too well. What's the problem?"

"She's rude and bad-tempered!" Maggie Rose flared up in her own defense, swinging around to face her uncle so she walked backwards for a few steps. "She called me Miss Uppity White Girl the day of the Celebration."

"Why?"

"I don't know." And the truth was, she didn't. Not really. For all Miss Sassy and her Indian friend knew, Aunt Olivia had told her to come right back. Sassy Face had no right at all to call her names.

"You must have some idea," Uncle Caleb said.

"I suppose it's because I'm white."

"Her folks aren't prejudiced. I can't see why she'd be."

"I guess she just doesn't like me then."

"I hope you haven't taken on my mother's foolish notions that colored folks are somehow beneath us," Uncle Caleb said.

"No," she said. *But why did she have to be here in the middle of a whole passel of them?*

Uncle Caleb sighed, and they walked the last few feet to the front door of the soddy in silence.

Throughout the evening she thought often of Uncle Caleb's words: *"I hope my mother's foolish notions about coloreds aren't blinding you."* Of course, they weren't. She would never be like Grandmother. Never! But that Sass girl was terribly rude and ill-mannered. She could never be friends with her. But maybe she should try being friendly to one of the other girls. Maybe Nellie Spooner— she didn't seem to have anyone to be special friends with. Nellie would be someone to talk to anyway. That is, until the railroad came and some white girls moved in, or until she moved into Prairie City next fall.

Tomorrow they'd be going to church, unless it snowed some more, and the road drifted shut. Nellie sat with her family just a row back from where she sat with hers. It wouldn't take much to turn around, smile, and say hello to the girl. And when Nellie came to school on Monday, she could smile at her again and say something. Maybe she'd say something about Christmas.

Maggie Rose could barely remember Christmas, before her father's death had stopped even the mention of it. There had once been packages wrapped in colorful, shiny paper —packages that held books and dolls and pretty dresses. Then nothing. Nothing at all to mark the day.

She had envied the girls at school who talked of parties, gifts, and new Christmas dresses. This year, she would envy no more. This year, she would have a Christmas and maybe a friend too.

Because trees were scarce on the prairie, and there were no pines for a traditional tree, Aunt Olivia said they would not have a tree at home. There would be a tree at the church, however. The men would cut a big cottonwood somewhere along the river, and the women would decorate it for the Christmas Eve services. "We'll open our gifts on Christmas morning," Aunt Olivia said, smiling, "and later you and I will fix a lovely dinner."

Suddenly, Maggie Rose realized she had no gifts for this family, for these dear ones who had so readily taken her into their home, and who treated her as if she were their own child. The problem occupied her mind for several days. All but a few pennies of the money in the small purse Mr. Foxworth had given her had been spend on food for herself and Hattie on the trip west to Solomon town. What could she buy with a few pennies?

A half-dozen times she opened her small trunk at the foot of her bed, as if she thought something might have been overlooked. But there was never anything there among her clothes, besides the few items she'd brought from Grandmother's: her mother's hand mirror and a small picture of her father—nothing she could use for gifts.

On Sunday, remembering her vow to try to make friends with Nellie, she smiled at the girl. Nellie flashed her a quick, shy smile in return, then ducked her head so low that hardly any of her face showed. But that was okay, Maggie Rose told herself. It was a start.

The next day at school, she asked Nellie how to spell a word she knew perfectly well how to spell. Nellie acted pleased to spell it for her, and at recess asked if she'd join her and the others in a game they played outside in the snow, called fox and geese.

That had made Miss Sass Martin sit up and take notice. The girl's big eyes got even bigger, and she poked her Indian friend and they both stared. It had been so much fun running from the "fox," even though no one tried very hard to tag her. Nellie probably would have tried, but she was never tagged either.

Maggie Rose was surprised at how much better she felt back in the classroom. She knew the fresh air and exercise was a part of it, but more than that was the feeling that in some small way, she now belonged. However later in the day, she decided that she didn't belong at all. No one but Nellie and Mr. Jacobs ever spoke to her. Of course, she didn't belong. She was white, and they were colored.

Christmas was on a Tuesday, so there was no school on Monday or the rest of the week. The Saturday before Christmas, Aunt Olivia had her pop enough corn to fill a large pan. Aunt Olivia set aside half of the popped corn to make long strings of the delicate, white puffs. The rest she and Maggie Rose mixed with sweet sorghum to make popcorn balls. The next day, they sat together and threaded the corn on red thread with the aid of small darning needles. The strands, Aunt Olivia said, would be used to decorate the tree at the church.

Aunt Olivia talked as if the whole community would come to church on Christmas Eve. Afterwards, everyone would stay to visit and eat a late supper together.

"Will that old woman, that Miss Julia Hardy, come to the Christmas Eve services?" Maggie Rose asked, remembering how the old woman on that last day of the Celebration had flown at her like a giant black buzzard. It still made her shiver recalling the awful feel of the old hag's nasty spit on her face.

Aunt Olivia shook her head. "No I don't suppose so, not as long as we whites attend the service. It's too bad she hates us so much. But we can't let one old woman keep us from living our lives. There is no doubt but her mind is addled, and whatever caused her to hate us so, is compounded by her mental state."

Maggie Rose certainly agreed with her aunt and was glad the old woman wouldn't show up at the Christmas program and spoil everything.

They were riding to the Christmas Eve services behind the gray mules, when Maggie Rose suddenly knew what her Christmas present to her new family would be. It would be a speech, or sort of one anyway. Tomorrow, on Christmas morning, she would tell them how much she appreciated them for providing her a home. And she would tell Aunt Olivia how much the ring she had given her to wear meant to her, and how it had helped her stop biting her fingernails. She would tell the little boys that she thought of them as her brothers and Sally Ann as her baby sister. She would finish her speech by telling Uncle Caleb that, in this house he'd built out of squares of sod, she felt as if she'd come home at last. She hoped they would be pleased with her gift.

The tree, set up at the side of the altar, caught Maggie Rose's attention immediately upon entering the church. She marveled at how the soft light from a row of candles behind the altar illuminated the tree and cast a warm glow over the room. But her pleasure did not last long, for the Martin family had come into the church behind them and Miss Sassy was with them.

"The tree always looks so beautiful," Mrs. Martin said.

Aunt Olivia agreed, adding, "Our niece has not had a tree at Christmas since she was quite a small girl, so it is a wonderful treat for her."

Maggie Rose smiled at Mrs. Martin. "It is really pretty," she said. As she turned back to look at the tree again, she carefully avoided meeting Sass's eyes.

The bare branches of the big cottonwood had been draped with cotton to look like heavy snow. Strings of white popcorn and dried apples, the bits of red peel showing for color, circled the tree, and scattered among the branches were red and green bows and tiny silver stars. The stars, cut from a shiny paper-like substance, glittered in the reflected candlelight.

The pew benches filled and the babble of voices dwindled away to whispers, as Reverend Michaels stepped up to the altar. He raised his hands, and a hush descended over the room. Casting his eyes heavenward, he began to pray and a murmuring of 'Amen,' 'Hallelujah,' and 'Yes, Lord,' began to accompany his voice as he thanked God for the birth of His Son born so long ago in Bethlehem.

The congregation's constant response to sermon and prayer alike had surprised Maggie Rose the first Sunday she'd come to this church with her new family. She could still recall, although dimly, the church she had gone to with her father and Grandmother before her father's death. It had been a quiet church with soft hymns and quietly spoken voices. These people not only murmured their cries of 'Amen' and 'Yes, Lord,' but sometimes stood and shouted, hands raised high and bodies swaying. She'd noticed her aunt and uncle never joined in and neither did Mr. and Mrs. Mars. She'd asked Uncle Caleb about it once, why they never shouted or behaved like the coloreds did in church.

He'd laughed. "Most of us white folks have built our religion on the idea that God is offended if our worship is less than stern and solemn. The colored folks have built theirs on joy and spontaneous expression." A smile lighting his brown eyes, he'd added, "I think they might be closer to the truth. But, although we recognize that their way may be as good or better, we are too ingrained in our own staid ways to change easily."

When the sermon was over, the choir came forward—Sass's sisters and her father among them. From the back of the room, Hattie and her Mr. Parsons also came up to gather with the rest of the choir around the woman who had played Mrs. Mar's pump organ at the Celebration. Now the woman raised a mouth harp to her lips and blew out a note. The choir hummed and began to sing.

Maggie Rose enjoyed the choir's songs telling of the birth of the Christ Jesus in Bethlehem, of His mother, Mary, and of the angels and the shepherds. Once Aunt Olivia shifting the sleeping Sally Ann to her shoulder, reached out to lightly squeeze Maggie Rose's hand. They smiled at each other, a warmth covering Maggie Rose like a cloak.

Thick slices of ham, dried meats, and fried chicken, potatoes, baked beans, a variety of pickles and breads, as well as pies, cakes, and cobblers were laid out on a table for the supper meal. Maggie Rose held Sally Ann, while Aunt Olivia helped the boys fill their plates. After she had them seated, she came to take Sally Ann. "Thank you," she said, smiling. "Now you can fill your plate and sit with Nellie if you wish."

She and Nellie found a place along the side of the church close to the tree. Although Nellie was shy when others were around, tonight she was quite talkative. Maggie Rose was enjoying her company, when she looked up to see Sass Martin coming toward them.

Sass stopped in front of them and in a rush of words, said, "My cat, Miss Muff, has some kittens. Mama said to ask if you would want one. You, too, Nellie," she added, looking quickly at her.

"We got lots of cats," Nellie said. "Mama'd not be wantin' me to get some more."

"A kitten?" Maggie Rose said. *She'd love a kitten, but would Aunt Olivia want a kitten in the house? Or Uncle Caleb?*

A frown creased Sass's forehead and a flush traveled her dark face. For a moment, Maggie Rose couldn't figure out what was wrong, then she realized she was taking too long to answer.

"I...I don't know," she said, stammering in her haste to get the words out before Sass took offense and stomped off. "I'll have to ask..."

Her voice trailed away, as Aunt Olivia came up behind Sass and, putting her hands on the girl's shoulders said, smiling, "And what are we talking about here?"

"She wants to give me a kitten," Maggie Rose said. "Would you mind? If you don't want it in the house, maybe I could fix a box for it in the barn."

"I think we could keep it in the house." A sparkle danced in Aunt Olivia's eyes. "We don't have much trouble with mice in the house, your uncle build it so snug and tight, but there's a few now and then, and I hate having to take a broom after them." Her hands still on Sass's shoulders, she turned her a little so she could see into her face.

111

"If the weather holds, would it be all right if Maggie Rose came over the day after tomorrow and picked one out?"

"I'll ask Mama, the girl said, "but I think that would be fine. She grinned. "She's anxious to be rid of them. She says she'll not have a house filled up with cats." The grin she gave Aunt Olivia faded as she turned to Maggie Rose. "We got two gray ones and a black and white one," she said. "Mary took the calico."

A sudden commotion at the door, and a rush of cold air, made them all turn to look. Maggie Rose saw Mr. Martin whisper something to Jimmy and then turn and go to the door. A bent figure in black shuffled in and the door closed. Every voice stopped and silence filled the room.

"Miss Julia Hardy," someone whispered into the silence.

Aunt Olivia moved around Sass, took Nellie's arm, and lifted her to her feet. Sitting in Nellie's place, she motioned the girl and Sass to stand close in front of them. Her blue eyes went as quickly to where Uncle Caleb sat on a pew bench, his shoulders hunched a little forward, the boys pulled in under each arm. Sally Ann, Maggie Rose knew, was asleep beside him.

Peering past Sass, Maggie Rose saw Mrs. Martin and several others join Sass's father, and soon a hum of conversation again filled the room. Several others joined the small cluster around Julia Hardy, and Maggie Rose knew they were shielding her from them and Mr. and Mrs. Mars, who had moved to a front bench. Mr. Mars' long, lean frame was bent forward as if he was examining the floor, and Mrs. Mars had pulled up her winter bonnet of green velvet to cover her bright red hair.

~ *Chapter Sixteen* ~

SASS

S ass stared out at the wind-driven snow swirling about the window pane and tried to push back a rising fear. This morning, Papa and Jimmy had taken the team and wagon to bring Cora home. She hoped they were safe at Gabriel and Cora's sod house and not out there lost in this blinding snowstorm.

Mama thought the sky had the look of snow this morning and had fixed Papa and Jimmy ham-filled biscuits and hot coffee to take with them so as not to lose any time on breakfast. Papa hadn't been the least bit worried. "In this country," he'd said, "the weather can change as fast as a man can shuck his coat or put it on again, so it may blow over and the sun come out again." But they had only been gone an hour when it began to snow, light at first, but growing steadily heavier, and within another hour, a bitter wind had raised its howling voice, turning the snow into a blizzard.

"They won't be startin' for home in this," Mama said. "Hope it stop soon, so's they can get home tomorrow."

Gabriel had come yesterday after supper to talk to Mama about Cora. "She's not feeling good, and sometimes she has pains, and she's got another month to go."

The last time Cora was here, Mama had fussed at her for still doing her work, even though her legs and feet were swelling and she was tired all the time. She'd told Cora not to put any salt at all on her food, to prop her feet up every time she sat down, and to get a lot of rest. "Make that Gabriel do the cookin' and cleanin', honey-girl. Food won't be fittin' to eat, bed lumpy and dirt gonna pile up in the corners, but most important thing now bein' that baby."

Cora had promised, and Gabriel said the swelling had gone down some, but still she wasn't feeling well and the off again on again pains seemed to be coming more often and lasting longer.

"You go on home," Mama had told him. "Put some things together, and Papa and I will come for her at first light tomorrow." She'd patted Gabriel's cheek. "Don't you be a-worryin' now, son. We'll put that girl to bed, and see if we can't get her to feelin' better."

Mama had meant to go with Papa, but had awakened with a ragged cough and a runny nose, so Papa had insisted she stay in, and Jimmy had gone with him to bring Cora home. Gabriel would come with them and go back tomorrow to see to his livestock. After that, he'd come in every day until ten days after the baby came, and then he'd take them both home.

Sass tried to picture her father and Jimmy in Gabriel and Cora's small soddy, safe and warm. The storm had moved in fast with the howling wind swirling the snow so thick and fast that it seemed as if earth and sky had become one vast, endless world of white. Worry nagged at her, whispering, *Maybe they started back, and they're lost in the snow.*

Sass took some comfort from the warmth of Miss Muff's body curled up in her lap. Although the kittens had all been given away, Mama had not insisted the cat go back outside. Miss Muff was an excellent mouser, and there had not been a mouse in the house since she moved in. That, Sass was sure, was why Mama was allowing the cat to stay inside. She wondered how Maggie Rose was getting along with the kitten she had taken home the day after Christmas.

The day they went back to school, Maggie Rose stopped Sass as they were going out for recess to tell her she had named the kitten Fluff. Sass had felt a kind of warming toward the girl, until Miss Uppity had just as abruptly turned away. She guessed the girl had felt obligated to tell her the name, since she'd given her the cat, but had no wish to be friendly. It surprised Sass that Miss Uppity had taken up with Nellie. Maybe she'd figured out that colored folks were people just like white folks—except some colored folks, she thought, grinning to herself. Miss Uppity sure didn't care for *this* colored girl, and that was for sure.

Maggie Rose came by herself for the kitten. She had acted kind of shy, but not so uppity. She had looked down at the floor quite a lot, but she had answered Mama and Hattie's questions clearly when they asked about her aunt and uncle, the baby, and the little boys. When they asked if she had enjoyed the Christmas program, not mentioning Miss Julia, of course, she said it was the best Christmas she'd had since she was a little girl.

Sass had heard her parents talking about Miss Julia that night as she started upstairs to bed, and had stopped to listen.

"When she came in tonight," Papa said, "she was searching the crowd. I wondered if she was looking for Miss Goodwin. I'm at a loss as to why she attacked her last summer." Sass heard him give a deep sigh. "I tried talking to her, but barely got a word past her raving about something she calls the Troublin' Spirit."

"I wonder if Miss Goodwin don't look like someone from back in slave times. Someone she build up a powerful hate for," Mama said.

"Could be," Papa answered. "But, in any case, I think we'd all better keep an eye on her, especially when Miss Goodwin's around."

Upstairs in her bed, Sass thought about her parents' concern. It made sense that the woman probably hated Maggie Rose because she looked like someone she used to know, if Miss Julia made sense about anything. As Mama said, the old woman was addled in the head, and there weren't no two ways about it.

That Sunday of the Celebration, she'd meant to hurt the girl. If Papa hadn't grabbed her arm, she would have hit her with all the strength she had. Of course, Miss Julia was too old to hurt anyone very much, unless it was a baby or an old person like herself. Maggie Rose Goodwin could have knocked her down or run away just easy as anything.

The girl had sure been excited about those kittens. Right away she'd picked out the black and white one, laughing when it licked her chin with its rough, little pink tongue. Later, Sass thought it odd that the girl had picked out the black and white kitten. *Or would she say white and black?* Either way, she now had a creature that could no more separate her white color from her black, or the other way around. Like people…like Mary with her Indian and colored blood, and Papa, whose colored blood had some white mixed in from both of his parents. And being her father's daughter, she, too, had some white blood, although, unlike Jo, she didn't look even the tiniest bit white.

But none of that mattered now. She could hardly think of a thing now, but Papa and Jimmy and Gabriel and Cora. The storm started to taper off by suppertime. Mama fixed hot biscuits and stew, but worry took away their appetites. The next morning the sky was clear, and there was no wind. They were all tired from a long, sleepless night, and Mama's cold was worse.

In the afternoon, Annie, Jo, and Sass took the shovels, kept throughout the winter in the back room for storms such as this, and dug pathways to the road, the wood and coal shed, and the outhouse.

A south wind the next morning brought warmth to the air and the icicles hanging from the eaves, began to melt keeping up a steady *drip, drip, drip.*

Going out to get a bucket of coal for Mama, Sass looked out over the snow-covered town and the still white prairie. Nothing moved. She sighed and went back to the house.

Late that afternoon, they heard a noise at the kitchen door and, flinging it open, found Jimmy removing leather straps that held wide, flat webbed boards to his feet.

Mama almost pulled him into the kitchen. " Cora? Gabriel? Papa? They all right?"

Jimmy nodded. His face looked heavy, worried. He unwound his muffler and, pulling off his cap, said his first words since he'd come home. "Cora started having the baby, and the snow came, and that wind. We couldn't bring them home. We made me a pair of snowshoes." He gestured vaguely toward the door. *Snowshoes?* Sass had never heard of snowshoes.

"Gabriel had started some," Jimmy went on. "Heard about them from Mr. Goodwin. Can walk right on top of the snow."

"Tell us about Cora and the baby," Mama said.

Jimmy took a deep breath. "I'm sorry, Mama." He looked down at the puddles forming around his boots. "He didn't live. Didn't ever even draw a breath."

"Oh...oh...I was afraid..." Mama's voice trembled. "Cora? She all right?"

Jimmy shrugged. "Can't say, Mama. She just lay in bed staring at nothing. Won't say a word, not even to Gabriel."

Mama frowned. "Do you think Papa can get her here tomorrow?"

"He hopes so. The snow's meltin' pretty fast now."

They slept better that night with Jimmy home and knowing everyone was safe. They were sad about the baby, though, and for Gabriel and Cora. "Poor Cora," Annie murmured. "She was so looking forward to that baby."

"I know," Mama said. "But fate—she put her hand into these things. Don't folks have no say 'bout it."

The morning brought a sky clear and blue and a golden sun to melt the snow.

"They is sure to be home today," Mama said. She stood at the window looking toward Gabriel and Cora's homestead. Hattie came up beside her and laid a hand on her arm. She did not speak, but looked out across the snow-covered ground.

Sass was in and out of the house all day, walking to the road and looking out across the prairie. Already patches of brown earth showed in the melting snow. But by the time the sun began to sink below the rim of the prairie, the air had turned cold.

Sass was outside when she saw a dark shape appear against the white landscape, and her heart leaped up in her chest. "*That has to be them*," she whispered to herself. "*It has to be.*" She watched the shape grow larger, and when she could make out the wagon and horses, she ran inside to shout the news.

For days, Cora lay huddled in bed, stony-faced. She would not even answer Gabriel when he spoke to her, and she turned away any food offered to her.

"Give her time," Mama said. "She be needin' time."

They had come home without the baby's body, and Sass wondered where they had left him. Finally, finding Papa alone, she asked.

Papa smiled a soft, sad smile. "I expected you to be asking," he said. And so she learned that the little boy's body rested, for now, in a small hole in the back of the soddy.

"Among the things Cora had sewn for him was a little blue gown and matching baby blanket," Papa said. "She dressed him in that gown and wrapped him in the blanket. He was awfully tiny. Cora had a small wooden box she kept handkerchiefs or something in," Papa shook his head, "I'm not really sure what. We dug out a hole in the back of their soddy to fit the box in and closed it up with the dirt." He sighed and added, "When Cora is feeling better, we'll have a service at the cemetery."

"Oh," was all Sass could say and keep back the tears.

The sun shown cold from a clear blue sky, and the wind blew hard and bitter cold, the day they gathered at the cemetery to bury the tiny baby. The whole town turned out, even Miss Julia Hardy, although she'd come no closer than the small hilltop some distance out on the prairie.

Sass knew the white people—the Goodwins and Mr. and Mrs. Mars—were the reason Miss Julia did not come to stand with the rest of them. She wondered if Maggie Rose had noticed the old woman, and if it gave the girl the shivers to see her standing out there looking down on them, like some specter or haunt with her long black cape flapping wild in the wind.

Cora stared hollow-eyed, while the preacher talked about God and her baby. But when it came time to cover the small box at the bottom of the open grave, something seemed to crack inside her, and she began to cry and scream. Gabriel held her tight, his own face a mask of pain.

Through tears, Sass saw Maggie Rose let go of Bennie's hand and wipe her eyes with a white handkerchief. The girl's show of feeling for Cora and Gabriel's grief filled her with an odd kind of warmth and brought a fresh mist of tears to her own eyes.

~ *Chapter Seventeen* ~

MAGGIE ROSE

The next blizzard came one early March morning. Maggie Rose woke to the cold, gray light and felt Fluff, a small ball of warmth, against her stomach. She smiled and reached under the blankets to pull the black and white kitten up into her arms. Fluff stretched, yawned and began to purr when Maggie Rose stroked her fur. In their bed, Robbie and Bennie still slept, their small blond heads nestled deep in the covers.

Maggie Rose found Aunt Olivia in the kitchen mixing up a batch of biscuit dough. "We're having another blizzard," her aunt said, "but it's bound to be the last until next winter."

"The wind sounds terribly fierce," Maggie Rose said. "Are you sure it's not one of those cyclones you told me about?"

Aunt Olivia smiled. "Those come in the springtime. May or June...usually."

Maggie Rose crossed to the window and pulled aside the blue-checked curtain. There was nothing to see but swirling white. "Snow, snow..." she muttered. She was getting very sick of snow and cold weather. If she missed anything at all about Georgia, it was the mild winter weather.

"Shall I cook some bran?" she asked, turning from the window.

"Please," Aunt Olivia said. "And set the table, too. Your uncle's out seeing to the livestock and working up a big appetite. He was muttering about it being March, practically spring, and having a blizzard so bad, he'd have to tie a rope to the door so he wouldn't lose his way." She gave a small shrug. "I guess we're all longing for warm weather and sunshine. Oh, there he is," she added as the door opened, letting in a blast of cold, snow-filled air.

Stamping his feet on the threshold, Uncle Caleb brushed off his coat before slipping out of it and handing it to Aunt Olivia, who hung it on a peg behind the stove to dry. "I turned the calf in with Polly and gave her and the mules extra hay, in case this storm lasts awhile." He paused and grinned at Maggie Rose. "No school today," he said.

The snow and wind continued throughout the morning, and after the breakfast dishes were washed and put away, Aunt Olivia set up her quilting frames. During the last blizzard Maggie Rose had helped her aunt with her quilting. She enjoyed sitting with Aunt Olivia while they sewed, sometimes talking, sometimes silent, but always with a warm, comfortable feeling between them.

When she grew tired of sewing, she read awhile. Fluff rubbed against her skirts or leaped up on her lap, always purring. Maggie Rose had borrowed a book of poetry by Henry Wadsworth Longfellow from Mr. Jacobs and had begun to memorize her favorites. She now could recite *Paul Revere's Ride* and *The Children's Hour* to the delight of Aunt Olivia.

Throughout the long snowy day, the little boys played together, for the most part content. For Sally Ann, being snowbound made no difference at all, and she laughed and cooed and cried as she did on all other days. Uncle Caleb sharpened Aunt Olivia's knives, greased their boots and shoes with skunk oil, and found dozens of other odd jobs to keep him occupied. The store, of course, waited through the snowfall, until the clouds broke away in the afternoon and the sun dazzled bright on the white expanse of snow. Then Uncle Caleb strapped on snowshoes and walked into town.

The snow left by the blizzard soon melted into the ground, and the rest of March passed without either snow or rain. In April and early May, Maggie Rose helped her aunt plant the garden and was delighted when the shoots of green, destined to become potatoes and peas, poked up through the earth.

Several of the hens began to stay in the nesting boxes in the chicken house. "Setting" Aunt Olivia called it, and when, some days later, the eggs hatched into baby chicks, Aunt Olivia moved each hen and her babies into a wire pen, so they would be safe from hawks and other predators.

Uncle Caleb came home one warm, sunny day all excited about talking to a surveying crew out near town. "They're surveying for the railroad," he exclaimed, a gleam in his eyes and a broad smile on his lips. "They said they expect the Union Pacific to be laying track by late summer or early fall." In his excitement, Uncle Caleb grabbed Aunt Olivia and danced her about the room. "Oh, my dear," he said, "this is a fine, fine day!"

The news excited Maggie Rose too. Now more white families would be moving in, and at last, she would have someone for a friend. Nellie was a sweet, though terribly shy, girl. But she was a colored girl. Still, this was her last year here, so if no white girl her age moved into Solomon

Town, it wouldn't matter that much. Next year she'd be in Prairie City at the new normal institute and have lots of white friends.

She overheard Uncle Caleb talking about needing a new school when the railroad came through this fall. "It's not likely, if we get a lot of new white families, that they'll want their children going to school with the colored children."

"I don't suppose so," Aunt Olivia said. "Too bad, but that is how the world is these days."

Maggie Rose wondered if Robbie and Bennie and Sally Ann, when she was old enough, would go to the white school. She hoped so. They shouldn't have to go to school with coloreds if a white school was nearby.

Sometimes thinking about going to the normal institute in Prairie City next fall and leaving this home, this family she had grown to love, gave Maggie Rose a funny feeling in her stomach. It was, she decided, how one must feel to be homesick. She had read stories of people pining for their old homes and had wondered at those feelings. Now she was getting a taste of it herself, and she hadn't even yet moved away.

Usually, though, she was too busy to think about it— with the chores she had to do and now the garden to take care of too. Keeping the garden watered and the weeds hoed was a lot of hard work, but Maggie Rose enjoyed it. Fascinated by the small green sprouts growing into stems and leaves, she could hardly wait to see the vegetables they would soon be producing. Aunt Olivia told her many of the plants would flower before setting on their vegetables. She wondered if they would be as pretty as the masses of wildflowers blooming out over the prairie.

Late one afternoon, Aunt Olivia sent Maggie Rose into town with a list of things from the store she wanted her and Uncle Caleb to bring home with them after closing. While she waited to walk home with her uncle, Maggie Rose ran the feather duster over everything and was at the door, shaking out the dust, when Hattie came into the store.

Hattie greeted her warmly, as Maggie Rose stepped aside for her to enter the store. "How have you been?" Hattie asked smiling. "The last time I was here, your uncle say you been helpin' with the garden work."

Maggie Rose nodded. "I am." She paused for a moment, thinking she would say how anxious she was for the vegetables to be ripe for the picking, when Hattie said, "I 'spect you heard I moved over to the hotel to work for Mr. and Mrs. Oliver."

Maggie Rose nodded. Uncle Caleb had brought the news home one day a few weeks ago.

"They've got a big garden back of the hotel I help tend." Her dark face glowed with a look of happiness. "Next year I'll be tendin' to my own."

Maggie Rose remembered the colorful flowers that grew around Hattie's friend's house back in Georgia. Too late to consider the day she saw them—the day Grandmother had forgotten it was Sunday and had screamed at Hattie so loud all the coloreds in that run-down place had to have heard every word—she asked if Hattie had helped take care of them.

Hattie's eyes twinkled. "Tended to them my Sundays off."

Maggie Rose felt the flush of embarrassment touch her cheeks and ducked her head. "They were very pretty," she mumbled. She lifted her eyes to meet Hattie's. "Very pretty."

"Why thank you." Hattie's smile widened and abruptly, as if she'd just remembered something that needed doing, she told them goodbye, picked up the spool of thread she'd purchased from Uncle Caleb, and hurried from the store.

The next day, Maggie Rose was surprised when Aunt Olivia opened the door, and there stood Hattie Smith smiling at her. Maggie Rose's gazed flickered from the colored woman to the buggy pulled up to the hitching post. She recognized it as Mr. Parson's buggy and big white horse.

The two women, one so fair and one so dark, chatted away like old friends. It amazed Maggie Rose how getting Hattie out of Grandmother's house had loosened her tongue. But, she sure understood why Hattie had been so silent back in Georgia. Just about anything, word or deed, could set Grandmother off into a fit of temper. Even she knew the less she was seen or heard, the better.

Aunt Olivia sent Maggie Rose out to the spring house to draw up some water, so Hattie could have a cool drink. When she returned, Hattie said to her, "Mr. Parsons and me...well, we is gettin' married soon. The Martin girls standin' up with me, and I'd be pleased if you would too."

Stunned, Maggie Rose could only nod. She thought of Hattie hurrying from Uncle Caleb's store, yesterday, and wondered if the woman had just then thought about having her in the wedding and had hurried away to ask Mr. Parsons if he cared if a white girl was in their wedding.

"Annie will be sewin' our dresses," Hattie said. A swift shadow crossed her face, sobering it. "Mr. Parsons drivin' me and Mrs. Martin and the girls into Prairie City in a few days. I..." she hesitated again. " You near the same size as Sass. What I buy for her, I'd buy for you, so's you'd not have to be troubled with goin'."

Maggie Rose wished she could say no. She didn't want to be in a wedding, or anything, with Miss Sassy. A warmth crept up in her face, and she knew it was spotting her checks with red. She ducked her head and looked down at Fluff, purring and rubbing against her skirts. "That will be fine," she mumbled.

But of course, it wasn't fine. She would be the only white girl and have to be dressed exactly like Miss Sass Martin. *Identical twins* she thought, feeling a rise of hysterical laughter, only one's black and the other's white.

Later, in her bed that night, she thought about the trip to Prairie City that Mrs. Martin and her daughters would be taking with Mr. Parsons and Hattie. Of course she couldn't go with them; white girls didn't travel with coloreds. Besides, they would have to leave town at sundown. Aunt Olivia had told her about the dugout where the coloreds stayed at night on their trips to Prairie City.

If she went along, which she wouldn't, she'd have to stay all by herself in that hotel where she and Hattie stayed last summer. Uncle Caleb had to get special permission for Hattie that time. A sudden thought made her giggle. *If Hattie or Mr. Parsons had to get special permission for her to stay in the dugout with the coloreds, who would they ask? The moon? The stars?*

~ *Chapter Eighteen* ~

SASS

Sass was excited about being a part of the wedding, but she wished Miss Uppity White Girl wasn't going to be a part of it too. At least the girl couldn't go to Prairie City with them to pick out the material for the dresses. She knew why the white girl couldn't go, but she wanted to hear just what Hattie would say, and one evening, getting her mother's permission, she visited Hattie in her small room in the hotel.

Hattie offered her some cookies and a chair and then settled down in her own chair and picked up the sugar sack she'd been hemming. Indicating the hemmed and folded sacks stacked on a small table beside her, she told Sass she would use them for tea towels in her new kitchen.

After she'd eaten three molasses cookies and they talked awhile about the wedding and the material for the dresses, Sass said, "Maggie Rose Goodwin can't go to Prairie City with us, can she?"

"Oh, my, no," Hattie said. "A white girl travelin' with coloreds? Oh, my goodness, no. We'd cause trouble for sure. Get Mr. Parsons in a whole lot of troubles. Run out of the country, even," she paused, frowning, "or worse."

A cold chill ran through Sass. She knew what the worse could be: Mr. Parsons might be beaten or even killed. She wished she hadn't said anything to Hattie about the white girl. Sometimes she didn't use the sense she was born with, as Mama often said about someone—usually her.

They sat in silence awhile; Sass took another cookie and Hattie kept stitching on her towels. Sass thought about Cora. Hattie had asked her to be a part of the wedding, but she'd said she couldn't do it. Not now.

"Do you think Cora's ever going to get over being sad about the baby?" Sass asked.

"I do hope so."

"Do you think she's trying to get better?"

A little frown drew Hattie's brows together. "We got no way of knowin' her pain, Sass. Could be her grief won't ease up 'til she gets herself a new baby. Could be, one day, she'll just come back to bein' happy, anyway."

Sass nodded as if she understood, but the truth was she couldn't figure out how Cora could love that baby so much, when she hadn't even known him at all. Sometimes it seemed to her as if life was full of mysteries—like how the people in Prairie City let them buy things in their stores, but wouldn't let them stay overnight in their hotel, or sit at their tables and take supper in their eating places. And why did they have to step down into the dusty street when white folks came walking along the raised up wooden boardwalks? And leaving town by sundown and staying away until daylight the next day? Why? Did they think they became wild creatures when the sun went down? And if so, why didn't the Goodwins and Mr. and Mrs. Mars, who knew nothing happened when the sun went down, tell them? But maybe they had tried, and those other white people just didn't believe them.

"You worryin' over somethin'?" Hattie looked up from her sewing, a soft smile on her face.

"Oh, just thinking about how we have to leave Prairie City at sundown, and in Solomon Town we can all be mixed together and the whites can stay as long as they want to." She laughed. "Unless Miss Julia's around."

Hattie grinned and then sobered again. "Hope someday we all can live anywhere we want, white folks and colored folks together, but sure don't be holdin' my breath, waitin' for it. I expect they find some other reason to hate, even if the good Lord was to take a notion to start makin' us all the same color."

Sass thought again of Hattie's words, as she walked up the street toward home. Hattie didn't think there would ever be a time when everyone would get along—regardless of color. She thought there would always be people like Miss Julia and Maggie Rose's grandmother. "But," she had added, "just 'cause they is, no sense we have to be that way."

Two weeks after getting the dress material in Prairie City, Annie had Hattie's simple white gown made, and in the next week, had cut out and basted all the other dresses. She would fit them on the girls next, make any alterations, and then sew them with her tiny firm stitches. When Maggie Rose came with her aunt to be fitted, Mama had insisted on Sass being there. It hadn't been too bad, talking to Miss Uppity. They had talked about the kitten. It was plain she was fond of the little cat. It even slept in bed with her. They had talked about the commencement exercise Mr. Jacobs was planning. Sass said they had never had a commencement exercise before, but the girl said they had them in her school in Georgia. It seemed to Sass that the girl was actually a little bit excited about that commencement program.

Mr. Jacobs had decided to hold the service in the church on the Sunday before Sass's thirteenth birthday on the twentieth. There would be a supper after the program, and the women, including Mama, were taking their quilts to the church. When Sass asked why, her mama answered with her eyes and lips holding big smiles, "You'll know soon enough, honey-girl."

On the evening of the commencement, Mr. Jacobs stood at the door of the church, smiling broadly, welcoming everyone as they entered. As they filed in to sit in the pew benches, all eyes were on the many quilts lining the room. In all colors imaginable, the quilts hung smooth and straight from railings that someone, maybe Mr. Jacobs, had put up along the walls this past week, for they hadn't been there on Sunday.

Mr. Jacobs had the five graduating students stand at the front of the church and began the program by introducing them to the gathering. Afterwards, he had them sit in the pews with their families. Besides Mary, Sass, and the white girl there were two boys—Joseph Cantwell and William Small.

Mr. Jacobs then introduced Papa, who talked about the railroad and the surveyors seen earlier out on the prairie, and about the new normal institute to start next fall in Prairie City.

"At present," Papa concluded, "we have to send our children away to Negro schools if they are to achieve any kind of a higher education. But when the railroad comes and the town grows, we'll build our own normal institute."

After Papa sat down, Mr. Jacobs called upon Mr. Parsons to lead the crowd in singing a series of songs: songs of freedom, songs sung in the cotton fields and in slave quarters, and songs that spoke of African homelands and America's promise, so long denied them. The songs often brought tears to those around her, and Sass could almost feel the presence of those many souls who had lived and died in the chains of slavery. With a heart full of sympathy for those who had gone before, Sass stood with her parents and the others in the community, swaying and clapping as they sang the songs of their people. Sass's father had explained to her why the white people did not clap or lift their voices in expressions of praise, joy, and sorrow. "They keep their emotions inside," he'd told her. "That is their way."

After the singing, Mr. Parsons sat down, and Mr. Jacobs stepped forward to speak. "I will tell you a story of a time long past, " he began, in his deep, almost musical voice. "The first slave ships came to the shores of America in the early 1600s, landing at Jamestown, Virginia."

The crowd responded with shouts and murmured expressions of agreement, as he continued telling the story of their history in this new land.

"Our people came with skills to teach the white man. We taught them to grow rice and sugar and indigo. We labored for them and gave our lives for them. We brought our own religions, our own heritage, and the white man did not understand. We came from Africa, from the West Indies, and other countries. We came from different tribes, with different religions and knowledge of healing. We brought our own colors and designs to create beautiful works for our own pleasure and use—designs and colors to tell our stories." He spread his arms and his gaze swept the quilts along the walls. "Not unlike these works displayed here."

Mr. Jacobs paused ever so slightly and then continued, "We sang at work and at play and danced our songs and worked the rhythm of it into our lives, for we weren't just singing songs, but giving lessons of life and the history of our people to our children. We stored our lessons, our heritage, in our memories, for we had no books or libraries. And to seal those memories, we sang our histories…our lessons." He stopped and stepped back, and Mr. Parsons rose to his feet.

"Our songs might begin like this," Mr. Parsons said, and in his deep, true voice, he began to sing: "*There flowed through the land a wide, deep river … green as new leaves upon the trees… along its banks there lived a people… a people whose chief was Kakatauh.*" Mr. Parsons sang of other chiefs, of famine, and of plenty. For the chorus, he had the congregation sing along with him: "*And the history of the people passed through the generations.*"

After Mr. Parsons finished the song, Mr. Jacobs again stepped forward and said, "We sang 'Oh, Freedom' earlier this evening. Did you hear the words to that song? *'Water brought us here and water's going to take us home'.*" His eyes swept the crowd before he spoke again. "This song tells of a legendary people brought on a slave ship to America's shores. They came out of the stinking, fetid bowels of the ship where they'd been chained, side by side, for days and days and long, long nights, without room to move and air too rotten to breathe. And as their feet touched the shores of this unknown land, they knew no freedom winds blew on this foreign soil. New chains would soon bind them, and the whip would again ply its misery." Mr. Jacobs looked over the crowd and, in a voice they strained to hear, he continued, "They knew there was only one way to escape—only one way to break those chains of slavery." His voice rose, deepening, "They would choose that way. At the water's edge, they turned as one and walked into the sea. With their eyes fixed on the far horizon, their hearts in the land from whence they'd come, they lifted their voices in song. Out, out they walked, singing, until the waves passed over their heads, and they were gone. Symbolically, they had returned to their African homes."

As Mr. Jacobs finished, a ripple of sound, a cry of mourning for those long ago people, swept through the gathering.

Then Mr. Jacobs changed the mood of the room. A smile lifted the lines of his face like rays of sunshine filtering through a dark cave, and he said, "For generations upon generations, we sang our history and told our stories. But we have a rich silent history as well—a history born of the struggle to be free of slavery."

He paused, and Mr. Parsons and Papa brought a wooden frame to the front of the room and stood back, waiting. Mr. Jacobs stepped forward and said, "The ladies will show their quilts now. Quilts that tell of our heritage, our history." He made a small gesture toward Papa and Mr. Parsons. They brought a quilt forward, unfolded it, and draped it on the wooden frame. The quilt was old, ragged, and faded with age. A soft murmur went through the crowd.

Mrs. Cantwell came forward to stand beside the ragged quilt. Facing the audience, she said, "My mama got sold off when she still girl-sized. Her mama, tears washin' like rivers down her face, give my mama this quilt. The new master seein' it special to her, or maybe 'cause then he don't got to provide no blanket, let her keep it. Mama growed up and brung a husband to sleep with her 'neath the quilt. Then babies they come. Some live. Some die. One who live be me. Mama keep the quilt 'til she grow old... 'til death done call her home."

"Thank you, Mrs. Cantwell," Mr. Jacobs said. "You did a wonderful job of telling your mother's story." He turned and nodded to her son, Moses, a tall man near Gabriel's age. Moses Cantwell came forward and stood silently, as his mother's quilt was refolded.

When the quilt was carried back to hang in its place along the wall and Mrs. Cantwell was seated, Mr. Jacobs said, "Mr. Moses Cantwell did not have a chance to learn to read and write as a boy, but he has an excellent memory, an ear for words, and a voice that will thrill you. He has memorized a poem by John Greenleaf Whittier, titled *Farewell of a Virginia Slave Mother.*" Mr. Jacobs smiled out at them and with a flourish of his hand toward Moses, he said, "Mr. Moses Cantwell."

"*Gone, gone,—sold and gone,*" Mr. Cantwell recited, his voice ringing out clear. "*To the rice-swamps, dank and lone. From Virginia's hills and waters,—Woe is me, my stolen daughters!*"

When he finished the poem, everyone stood and clapped and called out to him. Papa's "Well done, brother, well done" rang out with other voices, and finally everyone sat down again. Looking pleased, Mr. Cantwell went back to his seat.

The next quilt was Sass's mother's. It was a beautiful quilt made up of white triangles on a blue background— white stitches on white, blue stitches on blue. "Mrs. Martin's quilt is called *Flying Geese,*" Mr. Jacobs said. "It speaks to us of a freedom that Mrs. Martin, like many of us, was once denied. The freedom of the wild geese symbolized our own desires for freedom in those wretched days of slavery."

Miss Reed's *Log Cabin* quilt, finished in greens and browns, was the next quilt displayed. "In slave days, quilts were often used as signals," Mr. Jacobs said. "This quilt might have been hung out on the porch rail or the clothesline, or even a window sill as if to air, but it might also be there as a signal for a runaway. It could mean the master of the house, or the mistress, was back up at the big house or gone for the evening, or otherwise detained, and if the runaway was going to make the break and be gone, now was the time to go. It might also mean that there were others going with them, and that they would meet at a certain time and place. Other quilts with other designs were also used. A note, even if one knew how to read and write, could be intercepted, and a message carrier might be caught and the secret pried from him, often with torture. But a quilt, hanging out to air, was like a note or a runner that the enemy could not read nor capture."

Mr. Jacobs moved on then to an elderly woman's quilt. Using a stout stick to steady herself, she hobbled forward. Mr. Jacobs bent to whisper something to her, then straightened up and said, "Mrs. Jones calls her pattern the *Drinking Gourd*, or the *North Star*, a fixture in the heavens close to the heart of the runaway slave. The constellation of stars in the sky called the Big Dipper pointed the way to the North Star and often kept the runaway on course to freedom." Mrs. Jones tugged on his sleeve. He bent low, and she whispered to him. Straightening up, he said, "Mrs. Jones said she made this pattern from her own design and sewed the pieces in all different ways, so evil couldn't attach itself to the quilt." He bent again to Mrs. Jones' whispered voice, straightened and said, "There is an old belief among our people that evil travels in straight lines, and cannot manage twists and turns. Thus in creating this quilt, Mrs. Jones has blocked all evil."

Mr. Jacobs paused and examined the quilt more closely. At the center was a large long-handled dipper and in each corner a smaller, identical one. The elderly woman had made trees, clouds, mountains and flat plains in her quilt. "And see!" Mrs. Jones, caught up in the excitement of displaying her quilt, forgot to be shy and pointed to a ribbon of blue across a background of green and brown. "Right here's the water." Mrs. Jones was small, wrinkled and bent with age, but her voice came out strong. "The waters we follows to freedom."

"Yes," Mr. Jacobs said. "The streams and creeks that hid the runaway's scent from the slave hunters' dogs. Dogs!" he said, almost angrily. "Dogs, like *we* were animals." His voice softened as he thanked Mrs. Jones for showing her quilt, and Mr. Parsons stepped forward to help her to her seat.

"That concludes our quilt display." Mr. Jacobs said. "Now we will…" He was interrupted by a commotion at the back of the room, and Miss Julia Hardy, her black cape trailing behind her, hobbled down the center aisle. Standing beside Mr. Jacobs, she turned to face the congregation and shouted in a hoarse, angry voice, "I done seen the Troublin' Spirit! He be happy…He be dancin'. He be whirlin' and whirlin'… He be comin' soon! He be comin' 'cause of that one!" She jabbed a pointed finger at Maggie Rose. Her face twisted tight with hatred, the old woman spit out, "Get her out! Get her out! Get her out, afor the Troublin' Spirit come gets us all!"

No one spoke in the heavy silence that followed Miss Julia's rantings. Sass darted a quick glance at Maggie

Rose. The girl's cheeks were flushed, her eyes downcast. Suddenly Papa was taking Miss Julia's arm, and Mr. Jacobs was at the bench where Maggie Rose sat with her family. He said something, and the girl and her uncle left their seats and went out the door.

"She be gone now," Miss Julia said with a heavy sigh, turning to look up at Papa. "The Troublin' Spirit he done go back. We is safe now. The Troublin' Spirit done gone."

"Yes," Papa said and smiled at her. "I expect you'd like to take a plate of food home for your supper. My wife will fix it for you, and Jimmy and I will drive you. I imagine you want to be home before it's full dark."

Completely docile now, Miss Julia nodded and let Papa escort her to the back of the room. As they passed up the aisle, someone began to hum "Amazing Grace," and slowly the song grew. Sass knew the song had been written years ago by a slaveholder who had come to see that slavery was dreadfully wrong. She savored the words as they fell from her lips, *"Amazing Grace, how sweet the sound that saved a wretch like me. I once was lost, but now am found, was blind, but now I see."* They sang while Papa took Miss Julia on outside, and Jimmy followed with her plate of food. They were still singing when, a few minutes later, Mr. Goodwin brought Maggie Rose back inside. The girl's face was white as chalk. Sass couldn't help but feel sorry for her; she looked like she was only inches away from tears.

Mr. Jacobs called them back to the front of the church and handed out their certificates. Sass felt a small stab of anger at Miss Julia for taking her father away, so he could not be here for this special event that would never come again.

~ *Chapter Nineteen* ~

MAGGIE ROSE

Maggie Rose thought often of the commencement ceremony in the days that followed. The old woman had terrified her. She had also made her "mad as a hornet," as Grandmother used to say. If the old witch ever caught her out alone, what would she do to her? But what *could* she do? She was an old woman, and Maggie Rose knew she could knock her down if she had to, or run away. Surely she could run faster than an old woman. Still, it bothered her, and that night she dreamed of a black bat with the old woman's face. In her dream it dove from the sky, straight at her, screeching words that made no sense.

Several times in the nights shortly after the graduation program, she also dreamed of those captive people taken off a slave ship from Africa—those colored people who had chosen to die rather than become slaves, and had waded out into the sea, singing—until the water filled their mouths and the waves lapped over their heads, and she woke with tears sliding down her cheeks.

Mr. Jacobs had said the story was more legend than fact, but some form of it might actually have happened. The picture he'd painted with his words had been so real that she could see those people: those men, women, and children walking out into the water, singing until they drowned, leaving only the splashing of the waves to break the silence.

She remembered Grandmother talking about the slaves she and Grandfather had owned. "They were always singing and humming," she said, "perfectly mindless things, singing about everything and grinning all the time." *Had Grandmother not understood their singing? Were they not so much happy sounds, but songs of who they were and the history behind them? Had they shown cheerful faces to keep Grandmother from knowing how they really felt? Had they really come to this country bound hand and foot in the bottom of ships? Had slavery for all of them been a hated thing?*

Last night, she and Aunt Olivia had talked about the quilt display. "Mrs. Martin's quilt was just beautiful," Aunt Olivia said. "But the old, ragged, stained one Mrs. Cantwell showed had a bigger impact. Its story is so full of the grief those people often had to endure, and that, more than the beautiful ones, serves to better drive home the lessons of their past."

"Of slavery?" Maggie Rose asked.

"Yes—of slavery. I don't think we can even *begin* to comprehend the trials those people endured."

"Why do they keep bringing it up?" Maggie Rose asked. "It just makes them feel bad. Why don't they try to forget it?"

"It's their history," Aunt Olivia said. "A part of who they are, and they want their children to know their heritage...their stories."

"Weren't any of them happy?" Maggie Rose, helping Aunt Olivia get their supper on the table, paused in mashing the potatoes to look at her aunt. "They never had to worry about being fed or clothed or anything. For them life was easier, having no responsibilities. That's what Grandmother used to say."

"There's a partial truth there," Aunt Olivia said, picking up Sally Ann and sitting her in the little chair Uncle Caleb had made to sit on a regular chair.

A partial truth? She wasn't sure she understood. Adding milk and butter to the potatoes, she asked, "What do you mean, a partial truth?"

"It's easier to be taken care of, as far as food and shelter are concerned," Aunt Olivia said. "But many weren't taken care of very well. And even so, one can never be completely satisfied being totally dependent on the whims of another. And especially if they feel no obligation to consider *your* needs. Would *you* want to belong to someone and have no say whatsoever of your own?"

"No, I wouldn't. But I did, until I came here...with Grandmother," she added when Aunt Olivia gave her a quick look.

"It's still not the same," Aunt Olivia said. "Even if your grandmother had lived and you'd remained under her roof, eventually you would have grown up and she could not have held you then. There's no law that says a white adult must do as another white adult sanctions. In marriage, it is close. A woman is subject to her husband, which is why a girl needs to choose wisely." She smiled. "I trust you will follow your head as much as your heart when you make your choice. But I'm getting off the subject. As a slave, your family, even your life, was not yours, and as such was subject to the whim of your master."

"Like Mrs. Cantwell's mother who was sold off as a little girl?" Maggie Rose said.

"Yes. Could there be anything worse than selling children?" Aunt Olivia took a loaf of bread and began slicing it. "If we were slaves, our master or mistress could take Robbie and Bennie and even Sally Ann, sell them off, and we'd never see them again." Suddenly she looked up at the clock on the wall and said, "Would you stir the beans, dear, and then call Uncle Caleb in for supper?"

As Maggie Rose stirred the pot of beans, she mulled over her aunt's words. Something didn't quite add up. "Maybe we whites are different," she said. "Maybe the coloreds don't need so much to have their own say. Maybe coloreds don't love their children so much. Grandmother said the slaves her family had when she was a girl, and the ones she and Grandfather Goodwin owned, were happy all the time."

Aunt Olivia, setting their plates on the table, paused to look at her. "Those people love their children every bit as much as we love ours. They're not any different at all. Just in skin color. I imagine your grandmother was fooling herself. Life is easier if one doesn't have to face the truth. Now please, dear, run and get your uncle before supper gets cold."

As Maggie Rose walked the path to the barn to get Uncle Caleb, Aunt Olivia's words followed her. She knew what Grandmother would have said about that story of the people choosing death over slavery. She would have said it was a lie: a story made up to make white folks look bad. Maybe sometimes the coloreds did that. But Grandmother had said so many things that she'd found, since she had been here, not to be true, that she was beginning to wonder if *anything* Grandmother said had been truthful.

Hattie's wedding was held on a Saturday morning. The church was filled with bouquets of wild flowers and

MAGGIE ROSE AND SASS

a single candle burned on the altar. Maggie Rose thought Hattie looked quite pretty in her white bridal dress. She had known she'd be dressed in the same pale green as Sass, but she hadn't realized that the sisters, Jo and Annie, would be dressed the same. It made sense, though, as they all four would stand with Hattie during the ceremony.

She wondered why Sass's sister-in-law hadn't come to the wedding. Her husband was standing up with Mr. Parsons, and Mr. and Mrs. Martin were there. In fact, it looked like everyone for miles around had come, except for Cora Martin and Miss Julia Hardy. She sure hoped that crazy old woman wouldn't show up and start babbling that nonsense about a 'Troubling Spirit'—whatever in the world that was.

The ceremony seemed terribly long to Maggie Rose and, tired of standing so still, she shifted her weight a little. Her sleeve brushed Sass's, and they both drew back as if they'd touched fire. Sass shot her an angry look, and Maggie Rose felt her cheeks burn with her own anger. *The girl was so touchy!*

After the wedding, the men set up a long table at the back of the church, and Mrs. Martin covered it with a big cloth and set a cake, frosted as white as the cloth, in the center. Mr. Parsons and Hattie cut the cake, and each had a bite. After that, Aunt Olivia and the other ladies brought out bowls and platters of food and sent Hattie and Mr. Parsons to the front of the line. Since it was cooler outside, the men moved the church benches out, and everyone filled their plates and went outside to eat. Some sat on blankets spread out on the ground.

Maggie Rose saw Sass and her friend, Mary, get in line and farther back Nellie Spooner with her family. She would have joined Nellie if she hadn't volunteered to feed

143

Sally Ann while Aunt Olivia was busy helping at the food table.

Sally Ann tried to feed herself now, but she still needed help or else she spilled most of the food down her front. Maggie Rose was guiding mashed carrots into the little girl's mouth when Sass and her friend walked by. Mary smiled and nodded but Sass, (looking very pretty in their look-alike dresses Maggie Rose had to admit), turned her head. *Pretending not to see me,* Maggie Rose thought, and for the second time that day, she felt her cheeks burn with embarrassment and anger. Under her lashes, she watched the two girls sit down together on a blanket spread out on the grass at the edge of the churchyard. She saw Sass make a gesture toward the church, as if she were pointing out something, and their dark heads came together as they whispered some joke or bit of gossip between them. "Thick as fleas on a dog's back," Maggie Rose muttered, "And just as disagreeable."

Dark clouds began forming shortly after the meal was over and, with a fanfare of good wishes, the bride and groom were sent home in Mr. Parson's buggy. Everyone hurried to clean up and take the benches back into the church before gathering children and possessions into buggies and wagons, or to walk home, all with anxious eyes on the clouds.

"The sky's getting too black to be good news," Uncle Caleb said. "I don't like that greenish cast, either. It could mean hail or a cyclone."

His words sent a jolt of fear through Maggie Rose. *Would they have to go to the cellar? Could she stand the door coming down over her head, like the lid on a coffin?*

Uncle Caleb kept the mules at a fast pace all the way home. He stopped at the house to let them all get safely inside before taking the team on to the barn.

Inside the soddy, Maggie Rose pulled back the curtains for a better view of the clouds. Thick and dark, they rolled like muddy waters across the sky. *Oh, how she hoped they wouldn't have to go down in the cellar.* Just the thought of the door coming down over her head, made her skin crawl. Then suddenly, white stones as big as Sally Ann's fist rattled against the windowpane, and Maggie Rose drew back, startled.

"Oh, it's hail!" Aunt Olivia cried.

Uncle Caleb dashed in then, slamming the door behind him. A few of the hailstones came in with him and fell to the floor, melting.

The storm lasted only minutes; the noise of the hail slowly diminishing into silence. The clouds cleared, and the sun's rays shone from a bluing sky. They all went out to survey the damage. Aunt Olivia gave the little boys a bucket and they ran around gathering up the icy stones. Aunt Olivia's elm tree in the front yard that she had watered so faithfully looked ragged and tattered, the ground around it littered with twigs and shredded bits of green leaves. But Aunt Olivia was more upset over the garden. It looked as if someone had taken a dull edged scythe and mowed it down.

"A herd of buffalo couldn't have walked through here and done any less damage!" Aunt Olivia said. Her angry, bitter words startled Maggie Rose. She could not recall ever hearing her aunt utter an angry word.

"I know," Uncle Caleb said. "But at least we aren't farmers. We have the store, and we don't need a wheat crop or a hay field for income. The grass will grow up again, and I'll probably get enough hay to feed the cow and the mules through next winter. You can replant the garden. It may be too late to do well, but we'll get something from it. It could have been much worse. A cyclone might have taken the house, the barn, everything. No, we can handle a little hail."

Back inside, and much to Maggie Rose's surprise, Aunt Olivia mixed cream, eggs and sugar together, set the container in a bucket, and packed the hailstones the boys had gathered around it. She let it set awhile and then dished up small bowls of the frosty, sweet, creamy goodness. Lastly, filling her own bowl and sitting down, Aunt Olivia smiled at them and said, "It's an ill wind that doesn't blow someone some good."

Several days after the hailstorm, Uncle Caleb announced they were all going into Prairie City, as he needed provisions for the store, and, while there, they would look for a place for Maggie Rose to board this fall when she started normal school.

This time Maggie Rose enjoyed being in Prairie City. This time she hadn't just stepped off a train and wasn't dead tired with a soiled dress, her face and hair covered with soot, and the fear of what she was coming to hovering over her. They ate dinner at the Allyson Hotel and stayed the night, Uncle Caleb securing two rooms—one for him, Aunt Olivia, and Sally Ann and one for Maggie Rose and the boys. The next morning, they inquired at the newspaper office about anyone advertising for boarders.

They took the second place they inquired about. Maggie Rose liked the house immediately and was drawn to the young widowed woman and her two small children, a boy and a girl with large dark eyes and chubby cheeks. On the way home, she spun daydreams of living in the house, attending the school, and making lots and lots of friends.

~ *Chapter Twenty* ~

SASS

The summer winds blew in hot, dry weather. Sass helped keep the garden alive with water carried from their well and saved from baths, washing clothes, and dishes. When neither she nor Mary were busy at home, they roamed the prairies or wandered along the river. One day, farther up river than usual, they discovered a deep, shaded pool. "A perfect swimming hole," Mary said, and declared that here she would teach Sass to swim.

Sass listened with dread as Mary went on about it being far from town and any homesteads, and how they could swim without clothes and take turns keeping watch, just in case someone came along. Sass agreed that the shaded pool was beautiful to look at, but she was never going to go into it far enough to learn to swim. Just the thought of that water closing in around her body gave her the shivers. If Mary wanted to swim, she'd keep watch, but she wasn't learning how to swim, and that was that. Finally, to Sass's relief, Mary gave in and went into the water alone.

Sass sat up on the riverbank in the shade of a small cottonwood and watched her friend swim, marveling at Mary's graceful movements in the water. Heat waves shimmered on the prairie and after a while, a drowsiness settled over her. One minute she was watching Mary swim and the next thing she knew she was jerking awake, conscious of an odd smell and the wind rising up around her. She looked down at the river. Mary was out of the water, had put on her dress, and was sitting on the ground pulling on her moccasins. Sass turned back again to look out across the prairie. For a moment or two, nothing seemed out of the ordinary, then a puff of something grayish white rose up from the ground. At first she thought it was dust and wondered at it. It would take a huge herd of cattle or horses running across the prairie to make such clouds of dust.

The clouds of dust or smoke... *Smoke? It was smoke! A fire!* Now she could see the flickering red of the flames. She leaped to her feet. "Mary!" she screamed. "There's a prairie fire!"

Mary scrambled up the bank, her braids still dripping water. Her eyes grew big, as she stared at the wind-driven wall of smoke and flames heading straight toward them.

"Quick!" she cried, grabbing Sass's hand. "We've got to try and outrun it."

As they raced along the riverbank, Sass suddenly felt heat at her back and with a terrified glance over her shoulder, saw the clouds of smoke and leaping flames rushing at them like a charging beast. "Mary!" she sobbed. "It's coming too fast!"

"The river!" Mary cried. "The river! We've got to get in the river!"

Fear, a sudden monstrous thing, seized Sass, turning her legs weak and trembling. *Coming at her was the fire! She'd have to go deep in the river!* She felt Mary's fingers grab her arm and with a hard yank turn her toward the water. The fire crackled and popped. Smoke filled Sass's nose and burned her eyes. A quick glance over her shoulder chilled her to the bone. The fire was gaining! Tongues of flames crept out ahead of the smoke, running along the ground like fast-moving snakes. Another quick glance back and she saw a snakelike flame racing up behind them. Then, as if it were a snake, it leaped and caught the back of Mary's skirts and flamed brighter, hotter. Sass screamed, grabbed a handful of Mary's skirts and pulled. The fabric tore and the flaming piece of Mary's dress was in her hand. Stunned, her footsteps faltering, she stared at the burning cloth, dropping it as pain seared her hands.

"Move!" Mary was pulling her toward the water. Blindly she followed and at the water's edge ran in without hesitation. They plunged deeper and deeper into the water until they stood in the middle, water up to their waists.

Sass looked down into the water and panic rose, clawing inside her. Mindlessly, desperately, she fought to get out of the water and onto land on the far shore. They fell with their faces to the ground, Sass's heart pumping wildly. For a few minutes they lay there, gasping for air; then they rolled over and sat up. A rabbit emerged from the river a few feet from them and hopped away. Farther downstream, a deer stood deep in the water, motionless, its face turned toward the fire racing by on the shore, blackening the earth in its passing.

They got to their feet, their dresses heavy and dripping with river water. What was left of Mary's skirt hung ragged and blackened with the fire, but her skin was untouched. Sass's hand was red and throbbed painfully, but the water had taken out some of the burn, and it would heal.

They waded back across the river, Mary's hand gripping Sass's arm. As they neared the middle of the river, Sass's heart beat as if it meant to burst from her chest, and her legs felt as if their bones had dissolved. Instinctively, she pulled back. "You be all right," Mary said. "You made it once. You can again."

When they were finally out of the water, a new fear washed over Sass and she saw the same fear in Mary's face. *Had the fire reached Solomon Town?*

They ran, their feet flying over the smoldering, blackened ground until, in the distance, they could see that Solomon Town had been spared. Gasping for breath and with sharp pains in their sides, they slowed their steps. Close to the edge of town, they met Mr. Goodwin, Sass's father, and two other men who had hitched their teams to plows and had plowed a wide strip of sod, the grass turned under so it could not provide food for the fire. At the edge of the plowed earth, men, women, boys and girls still beat back small tongues of flames with wet gunnysacks and shovels.

"Sass! Mary!" Papa cried and running to them, drew them both into a tight embrace. Her face buried against his chest, Sass tasted the salt of her tears.

At home that evening, the fire was the topic of conversation around the supper table. Mama had bandaged Sass's burned hand, and it didn't hurt quite so much anymore. The fire had burned a wide swath—burning some hay crops and searing pastures. But no lives were lost, and Solomon Town had been saved.

They were sitting out on the porch, the next evening, when Peter and Clara Bensen stopped by. They talked about the fire and how close it had come to Solomon Town.

Clara Bensen asked if they'd seen Miss Julia walk toward the fire. "I was slapping wet gunnysack on the sparks, when she walk right by me, heading straight toward that fire."

"I saw her," Mama said. "And I saw you run and grab her arm, but I was busy beating at those flames flaring up and never paid no more mind."

"She walk calm as you please toward that fire and she act like she don't even feel me grab on to her arm. Her old eyes was just a-staring at that fire." Clara Bensen shivered. "It like she caught in some spell. 'Lord,' I say, 'what'll I do?' Then I turn her 'round and head her back t'wards her dugout. She don't struggle. Nothin'. The awful feelin' come over me that she ain't even inside them old bones of hers."

They talked about Miss Julia awhile after the Bensens left. "Too bad she won't confide in anyone," Papa said.

"Clara tries," Mama said. "But she don't say nothing back. Clara say it like she just look through her, like she not even there."

Thoughts of the fire haunted Sass for several days, sending little shivers down her spine at the thought of how close she and Mary had come to being burned alive. The river had saved them, and in doing so, had somehow eased some of her fear. Maybe she'd try wading out into deeper water, and maybe she'd squat down until she was neck deep in it. Maybe someday she'd even have Mary teach her how to swim.

A few days after the fire, they learned that they would not be getting the railroad after all. Mr. Mars had gone into Prairie City and had brought back the news that the railroad surveyors had recommended the train go south and bypass Solomon Town.

In his editorial in the *Solomon Town Gazette* the next week, Sass's father wrote of the town's disappointment. He urged them not to give up hope. They would survive. They had done the best they could, but some things could not be changed. He had ended his editorial with, "This is our town, and if it never grows any larger than it is now, still it is home, and home it will remain."

For days, the talk in town was about the loss of the railroad and the dreams they'd had for Solomon Town, but life went on as it had before and the talk died away.

However, something had changed in Miss Julia Hardy. Everyone could see that. Mama thought the fire had changed her—that she had seen the fire as an omen of some kind. Now, after talking to Miss Reed's hats, she'd stand in front of the white men's places of business, first the mercantile and then the bank, all places she has always avoided before, and yell that the Troublin' Spirit had come to Solomon Town on the flames of fire.

Papa said she looked like an avenging angel standing out there yelling, her cape flapping in the wind. Mama said, "She look more like the angel of death to me. She gonna do somethin', George. You mark my words."

"She's addled, no doubt about that," Papa said. "But maybe it won't last long. If we just ignore her and don't add fuel to her anger, perhaps she'll tire of it, or something else will register in her old brain and take her mind off yelling at the white folks."

Mama said, "S'pose she think her talkin' goin' to get them to just up and leave town?"

"It could be." Papa shook his head. "I hope she doesn't get the idea to go to their homes with her tirade."

"That'd need stoppin'," Mama said, "one way or the other."

Sass agreed with her mother. She had heard the old woman's ranting, calling the Goodwin and Mars families white-eyed creatures of evil, and Maggie Rose the child of Satan himself. According to Miss Julia, the Goodwins

and Mr. and Mrs. Mars had made a path for evil to come to
Solomon Town. But it was the white girl who had enticed
the Troubling Spirit. She was the evil one, and it was because of her that the Troubling Spirit had come, dancing on
a path made by flames of fire.

Sass wondered if Maggie Rose had heard the old woman, or if Mr. Goodwin had told her what she yelled outside his store and Mr. Mars' bank. She hoped not. The girl
might be rude and uppity, but she didn't deserve the terrible things Miss Julia was saying.

Sass knew her father had tried talking to the old woman, even going out to meet her at her dugout, but it did no
good. "It used to be," he said, "that she would listen to me.
But her mind seems to have taken a turn. All we can hope
for is that it will take another turn and she'll come to her
senses."

He was silent for a moment then added with a sigh, "If
she continues this, I'll have to go see the sheriff in Prairie
City and see what he suggests. I expect there's an institu-
tion for the insane in Topeka or Kansas City. They might
not take black folks, but the sheriff should know." Abruptly, he pushed back his chair and announced that he'd better
get back to the office or the newspaper wouldn't get out on
time this week.

Sass had once walked by Miss Julia when the old woman was screaming about the Troublin' Spirit and the evil
white folks. That time it had been as if she were invisible,
so she was unprepared one morning when she arrived at
Mr. Goodwin's store and, just as she reached for the door
handle, Miss Julia screamed at her, "Stop, girl. Stop!"

Sass' first instinct was to run into the safety of Mr.
Goodwin's mercantile, but instead she turned to the old

woman. "Miss Julia," she said. She heard her voice quiver, betraying her fear, "Are you all right?"

The old woman's rag-covered head bent, until her dark, glittering eyes were just inches away from Sass's face. "Don't you be goin' there, girl," the woman hissed through snags of yellowed teeth. "They is evil there."

Cold shivers raced down Sass's spine as she looked into those wells of hate. She stumbled backwards, away from the glittering eyes and the snarling mouth. She would have fallen as the door opened behind her, if Mr. Goodwin had not taken her arm to pull her inside the store.

"She's really going at it today," Mr. Goodwin said, as matter-of-fact as if he were discussing nothing more than the weather. "I think I've about got my share though. Soon she ought to be going over to harass Mr. Mars awhile."

"Papa tried talking to her," Sass said, fighting the sudden welling of tears. "She just won't listen. I'm sorry she's so mean. So hateful."

"I know." Mr. Goodwin looked toward the door. "It's not your fault or your father's, or anyone's. We can't control other people's thoughts. She reminds me some of my mother. She had no use for colored people, just as Miss Julia has no use for us whites."

Sass wiped away the dampness of tears with a hasty swipe of her fingertips before looking up again at Mr. Goodwin. "I think your niece is the one upsetting her the most."

"Yes. It does seem so. And I'm at a loss as to why. Maybe she reminds her of someone, or maybe because she yelled back and called her a few names after Miss Julia scared her so at the Celebration." He chuckled a little. "She shouldn't have, but I imagine I would have, too. Anger is a natural reaction to fright." He grinned. "But I bet you didn't come here just to listen to me, now did you?"

She grinned back at him, the guilty feelings she'd had, as if she were somehow responsible for Miss Julia's words—vanished. "No. I mean, yes. No…" She stopped again, embarrassed.

"Want to start over again?" Mr. Goodwin's gentle voice and twinkling brown eyes put her at ease.

"I think I'd better," she said with a smile.

Sass made her purchase for her mother, and following Mr. Goodwin's suggestion, was ready to leave by the back door, when she saw her father coming up the boardwalk in front of the store.

"Looks like your father is going to take another stab at getting Miss Julia to back off. Want to stay and watch?"

Nodding, she went over to stand beside Mr. Goodwin. Through the window in the door, she saw her father take Miss Julia's arm. With a conspiring wink, Mr. Goodwin eased open the door, so they could hear what was being said.

"Let me take you home now, Miss Julia." Papa's voice was calm, gentle.

She peered up at him as if trying to figure out who he was and then said, "Yes, sir, I be goin' now. Be goin' home." Without even a hint of protest, she let Papa take her arm and lead her away.

A few minutes after Papa left with Miss Julia, Maggie Rose entered the store. "I saw her," she said, excitement in her voice and the glow on her face. "Aunt Olivia said to not get too close, so I waited by the bank until Mr. Martin came and took her away."

She saw Sass then and looked a little startled. "Hello," she said. The excitement in her voice vanished and left it sounding dull and flat.

"Hello," Sass answered, then slipped past her and out the door. Outside, tears of anger stinging her eyes, she began to run towards home.

"Somethin' chasin' after you, girl?" Mama said, as she burst through the door.

"That Miss Uppity Goodwin!" Sass sputtered.

"Chasin' you?" Mama frowned. "What you callin' her? Miss what?"

"Uppity...'cause she is, Mama. But she's not chasin' me." The silliness of it, Miss Uppity chasing her, tickled her, and she giggled a little, the edge of her anger dissolving like a lump of sugar in her mouth. "I saw her at the store, and she went to actin' again like she don't like me. Not that I care," she added hastily. "But, goodness sakes, can't she act pleasant toward me?"

"You tell me she and Nellie Spooner gettin' along," Mama said. "So guess color got nothin' to do with it. Could be you two just got started off on the wrong foot. Why not try again?"

"How?" Sass asked.

"It's powerful hot these afternoons. Think she'd like goin' to the river with you and Mary?"

"I don't think so," Sass said.

"Won't know 'til you ask, honey-girl."

Sass knew that even if she asked, the girl would turn her down. Mama just didn't understand.

That evening Hattie, Mr. Parsons, Gabriel, and Cora came for supper. Cora was her old self again, thanks to Mama. At first, when Gabriel told Mama that Cora moved about the house like a ghost, staying in her long white nightgown all day and not even combing her hair or fixing anything to eat, Mama said to give her time. Cora did get some better, but not much. When spring came, she didn't show any interest in getting her flowerbeds ready, and Gabriel was still doing most of the cooking and cleaning. So Mama started having Jimmy drive her out to their homestead every day.

"Mostly I talk about the baby," Mama said. "And pretty soon Cora got to talkin', too, and lettin' her grief spill out along with her fear of maybe another baby dying." Mama said she told Cora they wouldn't ever forget their first-born child, and each winter when his birthday came, they would think, *now he would be one year old, and then two, and someday even twenty or twenty-five.* But no matter how many years went by, he would always be a part of their lives.

It had sure helped Cora, having Mama talk about that baby. She'd started smiling again, doing up her work, and now she was sitting with them at the table, asking Hattie about her flowers and if she ever worked wood ashes into the soil for some plant Sass didn't quite get the name of. But that didn't much matter. What mattered was that Cora was happy again.

Mama had told her, Annie, and Jo this story of Cora—not because she wanted them to think she had done something special, she said, because she hadn't. She just knew, and she wanted them to know, that grief can be a hard thing to get past. Sometimes a person gets stuck in their grieving and can't find their way out. But often, if allowed to remember and talk about their sorrow, grief would start to pick up its things and pretty soon slip right out the door, just returning now and then for a visit. "Visits we able to bear up under," Mama said, "It's the day-in, day-out company that soon grind us down."

~ *Chapter Twenty-One* ~

MAGGIE ROSE

An urgent voice calling and a banging at the door brought Maggie Rose straight up in her bed with fear clutching her heart. *Something had happened to the baby! To Sally Ann!*

She had been sick now for nearly a week, and last night Maggie Rose had gone to sleep to the sound of her whimpering cries and the creak of Aunt Olivia's rocking chair. *But someone knocking at the door? That didn't make sense.* In the pitch-black room she heard the boys stir in their bed, and Robbie whispered, "What's the matter, Maggie Rose?"

"I don't know," she answered. "Listen. Your father's talking." She strained her ears to make out the words Uncle Caleb was speaking to the person who had knocked so hard and loud at the door.

Suddenly, the curtain by her bed parted, and Aunt Olivia stood in the doorway, a silhouette in the lamp lit behind her. She held a whimpering Sally Ann in her arms. "The store's on fire. Jimmy Martin came to tell us. You'll have to go, Maggie Rose. Uncle Caleb said for me to come and leave you with Sally Ann, but I can't. She's so sick. She needs me. You'll have to take our buckets and ride Muley."

As Aunt Olivia stepped back and let the curtain drop back in place, Bennie's voice, filled with fear, came out of the darkness. "What's on fire?"

Maggie Rose answered him, as she felt around in the dark for her dress. Slipping it over her head, she tightened the string holding her night braid. Picking up shoes and stockings, she hurried out into the main room, the boys following her. Aunt Olivia had one hand on the doorknob, the other clutching two empty buckets. "Your uncle brought up the mules, and he's gone on Big Boy. You're to take Muley. Come on. I'll help you up on him."

Aunt Olivia had returned Sally Ann to her little slatted bed in their bedroom, and the little girl's whimpers had become full-blown screams of " Mama! Mama!" Aunt Olivia's eyes darted toward the bedroom, then she blinked as if shutting off tears, and setting her jaw, she motioned with a quick hand. "Come on, Maggie Rose."

The mule stood tethered to the hitching post, bridled, but without anything to sit on. She remembered then that Uncle Caleb did not own a saddle, but on the rare occasion he rode the mules, he rode bareback. She had never ridden a mule and started to protest, but Aunt Olivia wasn't listening.

Grabbing her arm, she pulled Maggie Rose around to the mule's side. "Pull up your skirts and give me your foot," she commanded. Aunt Olivia bent and cupped her hands, and Maggie Rose raised a foot to the cupped hands. Aunt Olivia lifted her foot, but so quickly and so forcefully, she nearly sent her sailing over the mule's other side. Only her hands, grabbing at its sparse mane, kept her from going on over. Aunt Olivia hardly seemed to notice. She held up the buckets. "Loop the bales through your arms and just give him a good kick and tell him to giddy-up."

Sitting astride the mule, her skirts hiked up above her knees, Maggie Rose kicked the mule's side. He didn't budge.

"Get!" Aunt Olivia yelled and whacked him on the rump with the flat of her hand. He jumped forward, almost unseating Maggie Rose, and started off at a trot. She bounced on his back, sliding to one side and then the other. And as suddenly as he'd started, he stopped. Maggie Rose kicked his sides. "Go, mule, go," she said, half-afraid he'd obey her. But the mule refused to go another step. She hit him with the buckets and again kicked her heels at his round barrel of a stomach, but still he wouldn't budge.

Through tears of frustration she looked toward town. Was it her imagination or was there a faint glow of red in the night sky? Maybe the mule saw it, too, and was afraid. Or maybe she thought, a dry, humorless laugh escaping her, he knows I can't stay on his back all the way to town, anyway, so why should he bother. She looked back at the house. They were only a few yards from the door, but Aunt Olivia had already gone back inside.

She dropped the buckets to the ground and slid off the mule. "Go back," she said. "I'll get there without you." She picked up the buckets and began to run, stumbling on the dark road towards Solomon Town and whatever might be left of Uncle Caleb's store.

When she arrived out of breath with a stabbing pain in her side, she was horrified to see the store nearly consumed in flames. From the big well the first settlers had dug in the center of town, buckets of water were being passed hand over hand, but they seemed to be making little headway in dousing the fire. Above the building, smoke spiraled up into the night sky, obscuring the stars. Maggie Rose looked at the buckets in her hands The line of men, women, boys, and girls, her own age and older, were moving their buckets swiftly along and seemed to have no need of hers. But she couldn't just stand there doing nothing.

She saw Uncle Caleb and Mr. Martin at the front of the line, and farther back, Mrs. Martin, Sass, and the other two girls. All moved smoothly, taking a bucket from the one in the front and swinging it back to the one behind, before reaching for another. Setting her buckets aside, Maggie Rose slipped into the line ahead of Sass and behind Annie. Taking the heavy bucket of water from Annie, she swung it around to Sass. With just the slightest hesitation, Sass took the bucket and swung it around for Jo to take. With the crackling, snapping roar of the fire in their ears, and the smell of smoke filling their nostrils, they worked smoothly, silently, until the screaming began.

As one they jerked to attention, facing the store, buckets halting. The screaming rose to a higher pitch, and out of the burning building staggered a human shape, alive with flames of fire. For a second it weaved and bobbed, a blackened form dancing with fire; then it collapsed on the ground and lay still and silent. Sass's father ran forward with a bucket of water and doused the flames. A horrid stench filled the air. Mr. Martin tossed the bucket aside and knelt down by the still form. "It's Miss Julia," he called, straightening up. "She's dead. Get those buckets moving!"

"*She's dead.*" The words echoed inside Maggie Rose's head. Miss Julia would never threaten or scare her again.

As they passed bucket after bucket down the line, Maggie Rose's arms began to ache. She wondered how Sass, or Jo, or any of them who had been at it so much longer, could keep up the pace.

Although it came as no surprise, Maggie Rose felt a jolt in the pit of her stomach when Mr. Martin called out, "It's going!" The movement in the line paused, and all looked to where Mr. Martin stood at the front of the line, the firelight playing across his grim face. The wooden framework of Uncle Caleb's store crumbled, and the whole building fell in upon itself, flames and sparks leaping up and then dying down to lick at what little was left for it to consume.

"We'd better wet down Miss Reed's place," Uncle Caleb yelled. Immediately the line shifted and the buckets of water were splashed against the millinery store. Several men with shovels ran to throw dirt on a number of small flames running along the ground, searching for new fuel.

By the time the danger to Miss Reed's building was past, the pale light of dawn was creeping out across the land.

They rested, some sitting on the ground, some standing in clusters. A ring of women, Sass's mother among them, seated themselves on the low edge of the well. They talked about Miss Julia and whether or not she had started the fire. Some were certain she had, but others were not so sure.

"It could be she just drawn to the fire and got too close," Clara Bensen said. "Like the prairie fire. If I hadn't stopped her, she'd have walked right up close to it."

Maggie Rose, listening, felt a moment of pity for the poor old woman and a sadness that she had died in such an awful way.

Her eyes on the tiny tongues of flames still flickering in the heap of ashes and charred wood that had been Uncle Caleb's store, she wondered what her uncle would do now. Would he rebuild or move on, maybe to Prairie City? Occupied with those thoughts, she did not notice Sass until she spoke.

"Looks like you got wet too," she said.

Maggie Rose looked down at her dress and back again at Sass. "Every time I swung a bucket around to you, it felt like half the water slopped out on me."

A slight smile erased the sober look on Sass's face. "And I slopped more passing it on to Jo. No wonder your uncle's store burned down." The smile slid away and left a concerned look. "I didn't mean to make a joke about your uncle's store."

"I know," Maggie Rose said. "I know you're sorry and I am, too. I wonder if Miss Julia started it."

Sass lifted her shoulders in a small shrug. "She could have. She hated your Uncle Caleb and all white folks an awful lot." She was silent a moment, looking down at the ground, before raising her head to say, softly, "The rest of us don't hate you, you know. "

Maggie Rose nodded. Sass didn't need to apologize for Miss Julia just because she was colored. Grandmother had been just as bad. Guarding the tone of her voice so it would come out soft and not somehow anger Sass, as she usually did, she said, "Miss Julia reminded me of my grandmother. She had no use for colored people, and not much use for anyone else. I don't think she even liked me."

"And you had to live with her," Sass said.

Maggie Rose nodded. "It wasn't so bad when I was little—before my father died."

"I'm sorry," Sass said.

Maggie Rose nodded. "Thank you." She hesitated, then added, "My grandmother was cranky and mean. I didn't like her at all." With those words, something flooded through her. *Relief?* She had dared to say aloud what she thought, and Grandmother's voice had not boomed down from wherever she had gone...maybe heaven... maybe not... but if heaven, than the Lord sure had a lot of work to do getting her fit to live there. "I guess she and Miss Julia were a lot alike," she said, feeling a smile lift the corners of her mouth.

Sass said. "Too bad they were both so full of hate. Papa says we ought to get along with folks the best we can, whether colored or white, so lines of hate don't get drawn between us. He says there no good reason not to live just fine, side-by-side, respect each other, and be friends."

Sass' words startled Maggie Rose. *Friends! Oh, how stupid she had been. Of course she and Sass could be friends. Mary too. And Nellie. They could all be friends.*

Suddenly afraid to say the words, for fear Sass would turn away or worse yet say no, but knowing she had to and even *wanted* to, Maggie Rose said, "Could we? Do you think we could?"

Sass looked at her, a slight frown wrinkling her forehead. "Could we what?"

Maggie Rose dropped her eyes. "Try being friends," she murmured.

She looked up and caught the grin that flashed across Sass' face and danced in her dark eyes.

But before she could answer, Sass' Indian friend appeared beside them.

"I sure sorry your uncle's store got burned up," Mary said. "Hope he's workin' on the idea of buildin' another one."

"So do I," Maggie Rose said, smiling at her.

Then all three girls were smiling at each other, and although a few minutes before she had been so tired she could hardly stand, Maggie Rose now felt like twirling about in a happy, little dance. But the seriousness of this night came back with a jolt when she heard a wagon and horses and looked around to see Mr. Bensen drive his team up beside Miss Julia's body, covered now with a blanket. Their faces solemn, the girls moved with the crowd and stood silent, as Mr. Bensen and Mr. Martin put the blanketed form up into the wagon bed. Sass's father climbed up on the seat beside Mr. Bensen, and the wagon pulled away—the horses's hooves and the clink of their harnesses the only sounds in the hushed silence.

As the wagon rolled out onto the prairie toward Miss Julia's dugout, the townspeople turned wearily toward their homes. Sass walked a few feet with her mother and sisters, then Maggie Rose saw her hurry over and say something to Mary, who was walking with her own mother. She saw Mary smile and nod, and Sass turn and walk toward her, a smile lighting her face.

"If you're not doing something tomorrow afternoon," Sass began, looking suddenly shy, "Mary and I might go for a walk by the river. Would you want to come along?"

Warmth flooding through her, Maggie Rose answered, "Oh, yes. I'd like that very much."

As Maggie Rose rode home behind Uncle Caleb on Big Boy, she thought back over the events of the night. The store was gone, but maybe Uncle Caleb would build a bigger, better one. She felt bad about Miss Julia getting burned to death in the fire. She hoped God would take her craziness into consideration when he handed out her eternal reward. Sass's offer of friendship had really surprised her. She sure hoped the girl wouldn't change her mind.

Uncle Caleb spent a week cleaning up the debris left by the fire. Sass's father, Mr. Parsons, Mr. Bensen, and others came to help him as they had the time from their own farms and businesses. Sally Ann was sick for another week, but at last her pale, wan face began to take on its usual rosy glow, her blue eyes brightened, and she was once again her happy little self.

Miss Julia was buried at mid-morning the day after the fire. They did not attend the short service. She would not have wanted them to, Uncle Caleb said.

Mr. Martin printed a story about Miss Julia in his weekly paper.

```
No one knew her past or why
she hated whites. We only know
that her anger and hatred grew
until it twisted her thinking
and may have destroyed her.
We feel a sense of sorrow and
pity for her. We are thankful
that no other lives were lost.
We regret that Mr. Goodwin's
store is gone. His place of
business was an asset to our
town, as is the man himself
and his family. We hope he
will see his way clear to re-
build and remain a member of
our community and, as always,
our friend.
```

Three weeks after the fire, Uncle Caleb and Aunt Olivia took Sally Ann with them to Prairie City, leaving the boys with Maggie Rose. They would be gone a day and a night.

While they were gone, Maggie Rose kept the house clean, made meals for herself and the boys, and did the outside chores. When she heard the rumble of their wagon returning, she looked quickly about to be sure the house was in order. Then with a sigh of satisfaction and pride, she went outside to wait. Robbie and Bennie came from their play beside the house to wait with her.

"Well, we made a big decision today," Uncle Caleb said, stepping down from the wagon and going around to help Aunt Olivia and Sally Ann down. "I bought the Allyson Hotel, and we'll be moving into Prairie City in a few weeks."

"Prairie City!" Maggie Rose exclaimed. "Move from Solomon Town?"

Uncle Caleb smiled at her. "Yes. I got a tidy little sum from the sale of my mother's house in Georgia and used that. The rest we'll pay off as we go."

"What about the store?" Maggie Rose asked. "Couldn't you use the money to rebuild the store?"

"I thought about it. But without the railroad, Solomon Town won't be growing as I had anticipated, and I know a man interested in buying this place."

Not so long ago, Maggie Rose thought, the move would have delighted her. But now she was enjoying her new friends so much, she would hate to leave them. Sadly, she faced the prospect of moving away from these girls she had come to know as friends, especially Sass. Somehow, she seemed the closest to Sass. *"Hard to believe, isn't it, Grandmother?"* she whispered heavenward and half-expected to hear a sudden crash of thunder.

The next day, as soon as she got the household tasks and other chores done for Aunt Olivia, Maggie Rose hurried to the Martins' home to see Sass.

They sat together on the porch swing and talked about the misunderstandings that, until these past few weeks, had kept them from being friends.

"Now, you won't need to have colored friends," Sass said.

"But I want to stay here," Maggie Rose protested. "I don't want to move to Prairie City. I don't care about some old school."

"Yes, you do," Sass said.

"Well, I kind of do care about that," Maggie Rose said. "But I don't want to leave you and Mary and Nellie. Maybe you could all come and stay a few days with me. Your father could bring you, and Uncle Caleb could take you back."

Sass shook her head. "Did you forget we can't stay in Prairie City past sundown?"

A flush of shame spread through Maggie Rose. *How could the people in Prairie City, people with skin like hers, have made such an awful rule? If they'd just get to know colored people, they wouldn't make such stupid, awful rules.*

"I did forget," Maggie Rose said, and her shame turned to anger. "But I don't care about that stupid law," she said. "You'll still be my friend forever and ever."

"You'll have new friends—white girls—and you'll care what your new friends think and say." Sass's eyes were as solemn as her voice. "It's only natural."

Maggie Rose knew Sass was right. She would make new friends and those girls would be white. They wouldn't understand her wanting to be friends with colored girls—just as she hadn't understood, at first, that colored girls were just like other girls... like white girls. But she would miss these friends here dearly.

A sudden thought brought hope again to her heart. "The Celebration! We might come for the Celebration. It's only a month away."

"You could," Sass said. A slow, soft smile touched her lips. "I might go to school, too. Papa's thinking about sending Jimmy and me to a school for coloreds in Knoxville, Tennessee. I wasn't going to say anything until Papa said for sure."

"But that's so far away!" Maggie Rose cried. "You won't even get back for the Celebration."

"I might sometime," Sass said. "Anyway, we could write to each other."

"Oh, yes, let's!" Maggie Rose cried, clasping Sass's hand in her own. Through a mist of tears she saw their hands entwined, light skin and dark. Then their eyes met, and between them a smile grew and an understanding that despite the miles, or years, or the ways of the world that might separate them, in their hearts they would remain always and forever friends.

BEHIND THE STORY

The place names, incidents, and individuals in this story are fictional. The setting, a small town on the Kansas plains in the 1880s, is based on Nicodemus, Kansas, an all-black town settled in 1877, by ex-slaves from Kentucky. Those early pioneers, finding themselves on the nearly treeless plains, literally dug in, making dugouts in the earth for their homes. As the years passed, they replaced their dugouts with above-ground homes of wood, sod, and limestone rock. That first year, they arrived in September—too late to plant crops. They survived the first winter only because a band of Osage Indians discovered their plight and left them enough meat to survive until spring. With hard work and perseverance they battled all extremes of weather, grasshopper invasions and other trials, and the town of Nicodemus became a thriving community.

Although it was primarily an African-American town, speculation that several railroads were extending their rails westward and at least one would pass through Nicodemus brought a few white merchants to town, hoping to capitalize on the projected growth. But the railroads bypassed Nicodemus, and the white families moved on, as did many of the African-Americans. The town faded—but never died. In 1996, with a population of less than one hundred, Nicodemus, because of its unique history, was designated a National Historic Site/Park. Each year in July, the town comes to life again, as the descendants of those first settlers and of those who came in later years arrive for the "Homecoming," or as it is also called, *The Celebration.* Some incidents in the novel are based on real events and experiences, or are a composite of several events. There really was an ordinance, in a nearby town, prohibiting African-Americans from staying in town past sundown, and a few miles beyond the town's limits is the remains of the dugout where they used to spend the night.

In this story, certain liberties were taken regarding the "Jim Crow" laws which segregated whites and African-Americans in restaurants, theatres, hospitals, trains, and other public conveyances and places. Those laws came into effect in the 1800s, but state by state and in a spotty rather than a systematic order, and they did not become entrenched until a 1896 Supreme Court ruling. Other rulings and laws pertaining to African-Americans were not standard for all towns. The town that would not allow any African-American to stay inside its city limits after sundown wasn't the only town to do so, but not every town had that requirement. The term "colored" was used in this story instead of African-American because that was the common usage in those days.

The story or legend of the Africans who drowned rather than become slaves in this new land has a counterpart in an Indian legend. The Singing River in Pascagoula, Mississippi, was supposedly named for a tribe of Indians, who, rather than submit to their enemies, drowned themselves in the river.

The college in Tennessee where Mr. Martin considered sending Sass and her brother, Jimmy, was the Knoxville College for Negroes, founded by the United Presbyterian

Church in 1875. The curriculum included high school and college level courses and normal training for teachers.

All of the characters are entirely fictional and live only in the pages of this book. However, Maggie Rose and Sass represent the many who have transcended the barriers between themselves and others deemed "different" to find mutual respect and deep, lasting friendships.

CPSIA information can be obtained
at www.ICGtesting.com
Printed in the USA
FSOW04n0502311016
26744FS